BREAK HIM

REVENGE IS A DIRTY GAME

BY NICKI GRACE

Copyright © 2023 by Nicki Grace

ISBN: 9798872519508

All rights reserved.
No part of this book may be reproduced in any form or by any electronic or mechanical means, including information storage and retrieval systems, without written permission from the author, except for the use of brief quotations in a book review.

Cold, calculated revenge is my specialty.

— Bree

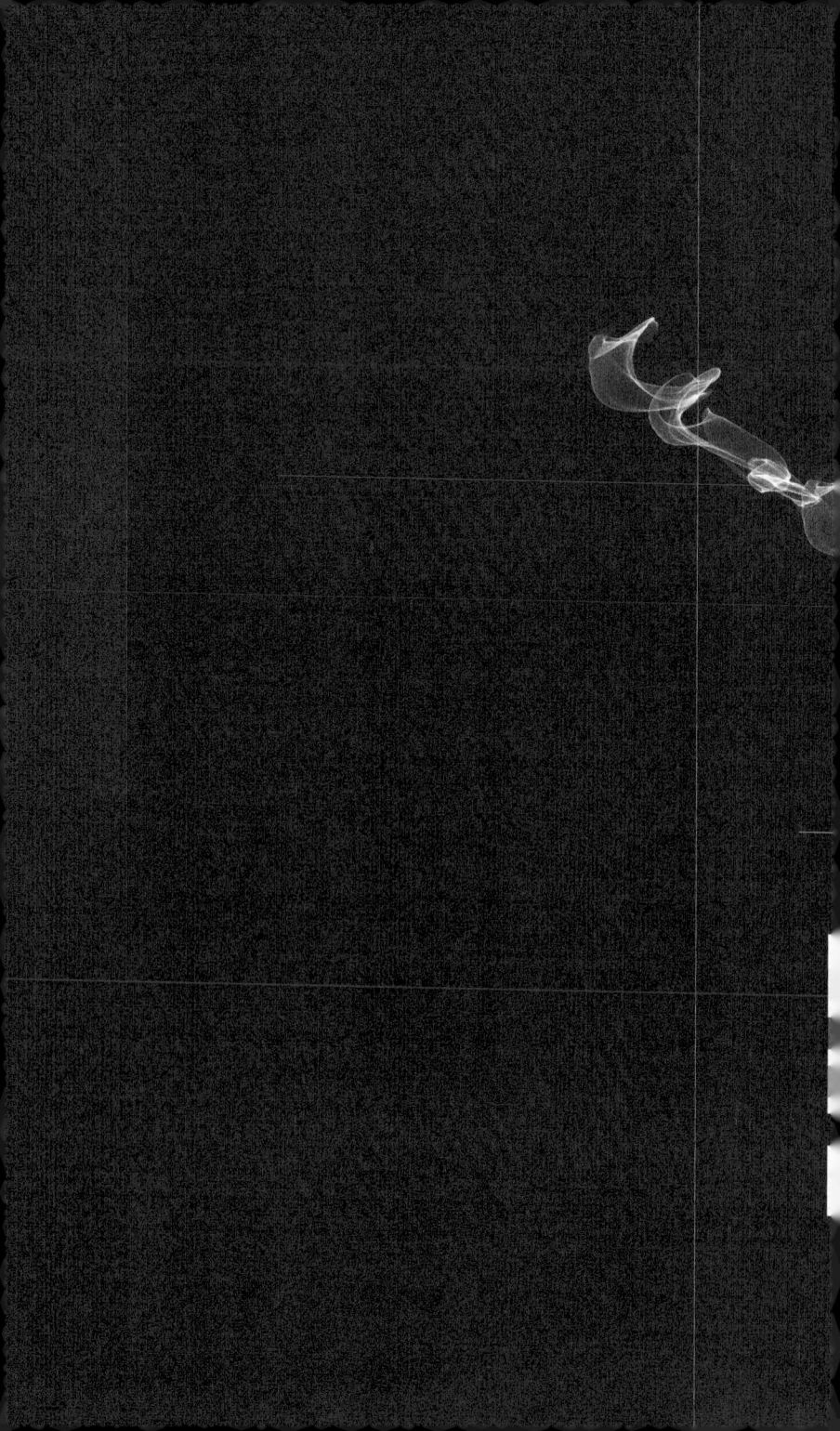

Day 1

SATURDAY
1:30 PM

I held up the box of condoms that promised warm sensations and sensual pleasure and rolled my eyes.

Elijah was at it again.

I frowned in disgust at how out of place the box was here, inside my carefully decorated and supposedly peaceful home.

Lowering it, my eyes immediately locked on the family portrait of myself, my husband Elijah and our three kids, Zoey, Grayson and Ariel, that hung on the wall.

We looked so happy. Only we're not anymore. At least I wasn't.

It's kind of hard to be happy and make beautiful memories when your husband's dick was roaming the streets like a dog without a leash.

I took a long pull on the cigarette I was holding and blew the smoke out of the open kitchen window, where I was currently tightly huddled.

It was truly a disgusting habit, one that I had kicked many times and typically didn't do indoors, but with how anarchic my life had become, I needed something with the effects of a tranquilizer to calm my nerves.

I only had fifteen days left. Fifteen days to stop my husband in his tracks and rip his fucking world to shreds.

That possibility brought a smile to my face. Or maybe it was the cigarette working its magic.

Regardless, I quickly put it out before one of the kids spotted me and I'd never hear the end of it.

Opening the box, I dumped the remaining contents out onto the kitchen table. Five shiny gold packets with pink bunnies printed on them beamed up at me.

Hmm. I'd never seen this kind before.

The new woman he was banging must have picked out these and from how many were left, I'd say getting hot and heavy with my husband was her favorite hobby. I guess I was just happy that at least this time she was over the age of twenty-one.

The last girl he cheated on me with was Leslie, a nineteen-year-old waitress that made playing my role of the naïve wife extremely difficult. Leslie called at all hours of the night, disturbing the small window of sleep I got before my then 1-year-old Ariel woke up.

Every time the phone vibrated its way across his night-stand, Elijah would quietly (or so he thought) rush into the bathroom and later tell me it was an emergency from work.

It was bullshit, and I knew it, but Elijah really thought I believed him and that was my fault.

For years I'd dedicated myself to his causes, took his words at face value and turned a blind eye toward every deceitful thing he did. I assumed he cared about me. If he didn't, why else would he continue to come home to me night after night?

Well, I now had the answer.

Because I was a damn moron, and if a person will allow themselves to be your doormat, may as well wipe off your shoes on them.

I shook my head and sighed, kicking myself for how idiotic I was, but thankfully I put that version of me to rest.

Payback for all he'd done was just the beginning. Therefore, he could keep all of his secrets, because now I had a few of my own.

My attention drew back to the condoms. I'd found them inside his briefcase, where he always kept them. I wasn't worried that he would get suspicious once he saw the box was missing.

Knowing Elijah, he would simply assume that he used them all and buy more. When they mysteriously reappeared, he would think he must have overlooked them the first time.

Fucking idiot.

A quick glance at the box revealed that it originally held twenty condoms. Since there were only five left, it seemed my husband had been a busy man.

And what type of wife would I be if I didn't match his energy?

I grabbed a straight pin from my sewing kit and picked up one of the condoms.

Earlier, I was attaching numbers to the Jerseys for Grayson's soccer team and now that my volunteer assignment was complete; I was free to do something more self-fulfilling.

Prick! I poked the first hole through the condom and utter satisfaction flooded me as the tiny needle slid through the packet, soundless and precise.

A devious smile spread across my face and if anyone saw me right now, I'd bet I looked like a lunatic admiring a precious jewel, but I couldn't help it. Elijah deserved to suffer.

After taking a moment to admire my handy work, I repositioned the needle to pierce through again.

Avoid the center, I mentally reminded myself. *Always avoid the center.*

Holes in the middle of the package were too obvious and raised suspicions. The holes I made had to be strategically placed, and I could insert no more than five per condom.

I knew it was unlikely that semen or any STDs could make

their way through these tiny holes. It was more so busy work to keep me from strangling him.

Prick!

You see, Elijah doesn't want any more kids. Honestly, he may not even want the ones we already have.

For instance, eight months ago, I took the kids on a week-long vacation to California with my parents. Elijah made up some excuse and stayed home. It didn't surprise me. Anything that involves too much time around us, he avoids.

Expectantly, he puts up a good front in public.

However, once we are in the privacy of our own home, the devotion vanishes and so does he — usually into his office where he doesn't emerge again unless he wants dinner or sex.

The sex I agree to, with condoms, of course, because it keeps his guard down. Initially, he argued that we were married and using protection was crazy.

However, once I told him that the type of yeast infection I get lingers in my body and could do major damage to his precious manhood, he agreed to use them and even stopped pressuring me for sex so much.

Win, win.

Of course, I didn't know if that was true about yeast infections. I have never had one, but Elijah wouldn't investigate.

As far as the dinners, I sometimes use that for acts of revenge.

For instance, last night's dinner was grilled chicken sandwiches and soup, which Elijah took to his office.

No worries though, I included a special ingredient in his "#1 Dad" soup bowl that kept him hugging the toilet all night.

Prick! Prick!

I should backtrack to explain why I am suddenly so angry.

First things first, it's not the cheating. I've dealt with that for so long, I'm actually numb to it.

Nonetheless, what I eventually discovered was a man that

cheats is a man who lies, and a man who lies, will secretly plan to divorce you, under false pretenses, after stealing your idea!

Prick! Prick! Prick! Prick! Prick! Prick!

Shit, I ruined this one.

Dropping the hole-filled condom onto the table, I tried to find my center by practicing the in-and-out breathing a friend suggested. It wasn't working.

My eyes locked on a particular loose floorboard in the corner of the kitchen, where I'd hidden a pack of cigarettes. Another quick smoke would be preferable to this useless breathing exercise, but I wouldn't risk it.

A breeze came in through the open window and I focused on two birds outside, that were fighting over something in the grass.

I guess even the birds were at odds.

Sweeping my bangs off my forehead, I relaxed my shoulders and allowed the cheery sounds of my kids playing upstairs to steady me.

Now much calmer, I picked up a new condom and started again.

Prick!

Before I wiped asses, dried tears, negotiated bed times and defused tantrums for a living, I was a technology geek in college on a path to having a very successful career as a software developer.

Fast forward fourteen years later and I'd traded my dream career for being a stay at home mom. I didn't have any regrets, but I'd be lying if I said it was the life I planned for myself.

I always thought I'd be the successful career mom that had it all, but in the end I couldn't keep up with the demands of a stressful full-time job and motherhood. Therefore, being a wife to Elijah and a mom to my kids makes up my entire identity.

That's why when Elijah came to me asking for my help to

create a software that would reduce the legal headache he experienced as a Sports Agent, seven years ago, I was happy to do it.

Not only could I dive deep back into the technology world, this would be my chance at reclaiming my husband's love and respect.

I knew about all the women he'd cheated with, but we'd been together for so long. Surely we could find our way back to one another.

Prick! Again, I was an idiot.

The software I created was ingenious.

It worked as a one stop shop that allowed athletes to access all of their past, present and pending contracts with ease. From there, the program broke down the complicated legal jargon into layman's terms so simple, even my seven-year-old could understand.

Last but not least, it included a feature that allowed athletes to evaluate the impact various sports-related injuries had on their contracts.

Not to toot my own horn, but it was a brilliant creation, easily worth millions of dollars, and Elijah loved it.

His original plan was to hand it over to his boss, Victor, to solidify a higher position within the company. However, after seeing the software in action, Elijah thought it much too good to hand over to his boss.

Therefore, instead of pitching it to management, he decided to open up his own sports agency, using the software as a major draw for clients, and we would run it together.

Prick!

The only problem was a move of that magnitude required investors, and unfortunately, as brilliant as the idea was, after a year of rejections, Elijah abandoned the whole thing.

I was devastated.

I'd worked so hard, and I thought securing this deal could somehow mend the tears in my marriage. There were so many secrets and lies pushing us further apart that I saw this as a major win for us.

In the end, I understood and accepted his decision to not pursue any further. As time went on, I had actually forgotten about the software and barely remembered creating it at all.

Imagine my surprise, six months ago, when I learned Elijah had secured an investor.

Six months ago!

That means I had no idea how long Elijah had been working on things behind my back. I'll never forget it. I was carrying a load of clothes to the laundry room when I overheard him in his office...

"So you locked in the investor for the software?" I heard Elijah say through the closed door. There was a pause and then he added. *"That's excellent news. And he is going to invest the entire amount to partner with us?"*

Us? I thought to myself, still remembering the spark of excitement that filled me.

It looked like Elijah had found someone after all and was going to surprise me with the news.

I stepped closer to the door, tightening my grip on the laundry basket.

Elijah's voice became stern and dismissive.

"I told you, Bree will not be a problem. She doesn't know that we were still looking for investors or that I have finally found one."

We?

My heart somehow raced and stopped at the same time, and my body was assaulted with an ineffable pain that shattered me from the inside out.

I stared at the door, my thoughts absorbed by disbelief and shock while the basket trembled in my hands.

But if I thought that was the worst thing I would hear. I obviously didn't know my husband at all.

"I have the original software in a safe place and have already hired someone to rebuild it through their system so that Bree can't prove she created it. Plus, I plan to leave her before the deal is final."

It was hard to stay upright and tears burned my eyes. He didn't have to do this. Yet he was.

I heard Elijah laugh. He may as well have been laughing directly in my face because I could see him in my mind's eye, clear as day.

The person on the phone must have asked why he wanted to divorce me before and not after, because Elijah said, "I don't want the money from the deal to be considered in the divorce. And any retaliation from her will look like lies from a pathetic woman grasping at straws and in denial that her husband no longer wants her."

I gasped, and the basket fell from my hands.

"Hold on a second." I heard Elijah say.

Quickly, I gathered the fallen clothes and rushed down the hall, turning the corner just as I heard his office door opening.

I blinked a few times, coming back to the present, staring at the condom in my hand. The pain of betrayal was still fresh and at the time I couldn't elucidate my feelings, but now I can.

I am done being his step stool, his constant support, and his naïve wife. The only thing I feel towards Elijah is anger and an incessant need to beat him at his own game before the clock runs out.

Prick! Prick! I withdrew the needle and checked over my work, mentally patting myself on the back for a job well done.

After placing the newly redesigned condom back into the box, I was reaching for another when my cell phone chimed, indicating a text message.

> Nicole: Elijah is here again 🙄... with her. That man is fucking scum!!!!

I watched the three gray dots bounce steadily on the screen. Clearly, Nicole needed a few minutes to get her temper under control. Finally, her next message sprung in.

> Nicole: I will forward you the pictures when I get the chance. Do you need me to do anything else?

I thought about it. The pictures would be enough. Besides, I also had a private investigator on the case.

> Me: No. That's all I need.

Thank God for Nicole Walls. She was the mom of one of Zoey's close friends and she helped me keep an eye on my bastard of a husband. I swear, with all the documenting I did, I was practically performing my divorce lawyer's job for him.

A wave of footsteps could be heard rushing downstairs, forcing me to hide my revenge activity. The footsteps carried a level of excitement and joy, suggesting that they were on a mission. That meant it was Grayson, my seven-year-old.

If it were Zoey, my thirteen-year-old, the footsteps would be loud and moody, like the world owed her something and she was coming downstairs to collect.

And if it were my three-year-old Ariel, I wouldn't hear anything at all, because she liked to slide down the stairs. It wasn't because she couldn't walk down them safely, but sliding was easier and a whole lot sneakier.

"Mommy! Mommy! Mommy!" Grayson shouted, with way too much enthusiasm for my dismal mood.

Despite that, his deep dimples and bright eyes made not smiling back impossible. He was the sweetest of all my kids.

"What's eight plus two?" he asked.

"Umm, is it ten?" I said, pretending not to be sure.

Grayson gave me two thumbs up. "Right! And what is ten plus seven?"

I placed a finger on my chin and thought about it. "Fifteen, maybe?"

"Mom!" he pouted. "We go over this every day. It's seventeen."

"Oh, that's right," I replied, tapping myself upside the head.

"Okay, and what's seventeen plus twenty-two?" Grayson asked, getting back down to business.

This time, my response carried much more confidence. I even puffed up my chest and placed my hands on my hips.

"Thirty-nine."

"Correct!" Grayson said. "And you know what that means?"

"We're the best super spies ever!" We shouted in unison, and Grayson ran off.

Grayson's favorite TV show was about a spy that solved crimes by doing math equations.

Every Saturday he watched it on TV and once the show ended, he came to me with math problems to solve. The exact same math problems might I add.

Every. Single. Time.

It would be nice if he would at least give me some new equations, but he was always so adamant about it and proud of himself that I couldn't complain.

I watched Grayson half gallop, half karate kick away. After ensuring he was in the living room, I reached for the condoms.

However, I was once again cut short by a light knocking on my kitchen window.

I looked up to see my neighbor and close friend Gianna Bianchi.

"Hey," Gianna whispered through the open window. "Open the door."

Her messy bun flopped from side to side as she frantically pointed to the backdoor.

After I unlocked it, Gianna rushed inside, almost knocking me over with both her erratic movements and an overwhelming scent of perfume. She wore a yellow tennis skirt, an orange tank top and a blue jean jacket.

I took a step back, watching her push the door closed and lock it.

"Are you being chased?" I asked, amused.

"May as well be. I turned on a TV show to keep the handcuffs busy and had to haul ass over here before they noticed."

"You didn't leave them alone, did you?"

I could never be too sure what Gianna would or wouldn't do.

Gianna rolled her eyes. "Matteo's there. Napping as usual. He can get his ass up and entertain them if need be."

Matteo was Gianna's husband and "The Handcuffs" were the nicknames Gianna had given to her four-year-old twins, Lucia and Gia. They were super cute but also super clingy.

Gianna scrunched up her nose and placed a hand on my shoulder, finally catching her breath.

"Excuse the smell, they had me playing dress up and, as usual, I was the dummy in both senses of the word. One for letting them use me like a mannequin, and two for being a klutz and spilling the entire bottle of perfume on myself."

"Yikes." I shook my head and laughed.

Gianna looked over my shoulder towards the living room. "Where's Pam?"

Pam was my cousin and, like Gianna, she was helping me get through the load of shit I'd found myself in with Elijah.

"She texted me and said she would be here in like an hour. There were some last-minute patients to take care of."

"God bless her," Gianna said. "I could never be a nurse.

It's too much give and not enough take. I get enough of that at home."

"I wholeheartedly agree."

Gianna took a seat at the kitchen table, and her lips curled into a mischievous smile.

"What were you doing?" She asked, nosily glancing around. "Please tell me it's something to make Elijah's life a living hell?"

Taking a seat at the furthest end of the table to escape the overpowering rosy scent she was emitting, I lifted the small towel on the table to reveal the condoms.

If possible, Gianna's grin got wider. She loved those drama-filled TV shows about out-of-control housewives. Deceitful setups and revenge were her middle name.

I preferred the classics where the female sleuths always outwits the bad guy.

"Oh, can I help?" she said, clapping her hands together and bouncing around. The act definitely made her look like the teenager her kids had dressed her up to be.

I stared at her in disbelief. "No, you may not! The last time you helped me, you ruined too many."

"I can't help it, I'm Italian. I'm passionate about everything I do." She held up a finger as she listed them. "Fucking, cooking, loving and hating."

I waved a finger at her. "You're not going to use that Italian excuse on me this time."

Gianna crossed her arms. "You're no fun. At least give me some good news. Did you find it yet?"

The "it" she was referring to was my software. Or at least, paperwork pertaining to the deal Elijah had with the investor and new programmer.

I needed it, not just to undo all he had built, but as evidence to prove to my lawyer just how surreptitious and vile Elijah was.

I tossed the towel back over the condoms and gave her a slight shake of the head. "Nope."

"None of it?"

I shook my head again.

"Dammit," Gianna said a little too loud.

She instantly covered her mouth, remembering that young, impressionable ears were around.

I waved a hand. I'd said worse.

Gianna covered her face with her hand, and then immediately backed up and gagged. Apparently, she'd accidentally taken a deep whiff of perfume. She yanked off her jacket and tossed it on the floor by the back door.

Breathing easier, she faced me and said, "Bree, we are running out of time and places to look."

"I know, but it's here somewhere," I muttered, looking around. "I'm just missing it."

Already I had searched his office, the kitchen, all the bedrooms and bathrooms. The only places left were the living room, the outdoor shed, and the attic.

"Maybe it was here, but it isn't anymore. Did you hear him say it on the recording that it's still here?"

I mentally groaned. *That damn recorder.*

I'd learned a lot of disgusting and unbelievable things through the small device I had managed to sneak into Elijah's office, and it all destroyed me every time.

It was hard to fathom the lengths he had gone to, the deceitful things he was currently doing, and the inconceivable actions he was planning.

However, as informative as my spying was, it was also draining and time consuming.

Between picking the lock, finding a good place to hide it, getting back out without the kids seeing me, and then repeating the process all over again to listen to what it had recorded and reset the device, I had almost abandoned the entire idea several times.

It would have been nice if I could get an actual camera set up in there, but I couldn't figure out a place that would be appropriately inconspicuous.

We sat in a sullen silence before I finally confessed. "I haven't snuck the recorder back in his office."

"What?!" Gianna exclaimed. "It's been almost a week. You could be missing out on valuable information."

"I know but, it's not exactly easy."

Gianna cooled her spicy Italian heels a little and placed a hand with colorful fingernails on the table.

"Alright, I get it, but that means that he may have already signed with the investor and destroyed the original."

She had a good point, but it had to be here. I was sure of it.

"If Elijah is nothing else, he is predictable."

The look Gianna gave me had me backtracking to explain my response.

"The irony of what I just said isn't lost on me, okay? But just because I wasn't able to predict that he was going to double-cross me, doesn't mean he isn't predictable. Actually," I said, my voice lowering. "I just didn't consider he would sink this low."

Gianna gave me a pitying look and tried to touch my hand, but I moved out of her grasp at the last second. I didn't need consoling. Maybe a cigarette, but not consoling.

"The point is," I said. "In some twisted way, this level of deception is the exact predictability I am talking about. Elijah has always looked out for himself."

"I hear you, but how does that prove it's in the house?"

"Throughout our entire marriage, if Elijah cared about something, usually business related, he kept it close. It was like he believed if he didn't have access to it at all hours of the day, it would get destroyed or someone would take it from him."

Gianna still wasn't convinced.

I threw up my hands. "His paranoia is the entire reason we built his home office. The man didn't even trust his contracts to be at work. So he brought the originals home and took copies to work."

"Isn't that against company policy?" Gianna asked.

I shrugged. "Who the hell knows? He did it anyway. All the while mumbling something about the agency could accidentally catch on fire, or worse. The man is obsessed with the belief that he will get screwed if he isn't careful."

Gianna laughed.

"Hmm, well, in this case, that dumbass is right. He should have extended that paranoia to things outside of business."

"When you are as money hungry as he is, there is no room to consider anything or anyone else."

Gianna nodded before releasing a long breath.

Oh no, here it comes.

"Everything you said makes sense, Bree, and maybe you're right, it is here somewhere, but maybe," she stressed the word. "you should just let it all go. Let Elijah have the money and the company. I'm sure he will have to pay something in the divorce even if it's only child support. Just cut your losses and move on."

Yup. The handcuffs had tied her hair too tight again.

For the last two weeks, Gianna had been getting more and more nervous. She didn't want time to run out and Elijah to file the divorce papers and walk out on me.

But If I told her once, I would tell her a million times. I would even the score with Elijah or die trying.

"I know!" she said, snapping her fingers. "You can recreate the software."

The woman had gone mad.

Recreating the software would be a time-consuming nightmare. There were too many variables. I was not putting myself through that again.

No, I would find my original software with all the bells and whistles, and that was that.

"Gianna, I am not recreating that damn software, and this is not about money. This is about making that bastard pay for what he has done. I am not turning the other cheek anymore. I have done it my entire marriage. He will suffer."

Gianna's concerned face transformed as her inner chaos lover jumped back to the forefront. She lived for this shit. The drama, the secrets, the spying.

"You're so badass these days," she complimented. "Very different from the woman you were when you moved in ten years ago."

I nodded in agreement, then glanced toward the living room. Ariel was walking by wearing a pink swimsuit and a sparkly green tutu, dragging her brother's yellow plastic bat.

Narrowing my eyes, I contemplated going to stop her. It was always hard to tell if Ariel was coming from, or on her way to get into trouble.

Come to think of it, Ariel would make a better ninja than Grayson. Then again, he had more honor and dedication to it because while Grayson's mission was to save the world; I think Ariel's goal was to destroy it.

I decided to let Ariel be.

"Elijah is out with a new woman," I said, turning to Gianna.

"A new one! Seriously?! Wow, if my husband was parking his cazzo in all these different women. I don't think I'd be so calm. Have you found out who she is this time?"

"Not yet."

Now that was a lie. I was always lying these days. Half the time I even lied to myself. I found it helped me stay in character and I was going to need to be one hell of an actress to pull this off.

I'd like to say it's all Elijah's fault, but at this point, it takes two to tango.

My phone chimed again, and I braced myself, assuming it was more info from Nicole, but it wasn't. This message I welcomed. In fact, I needed it.

> R: Hey Love, I'm missing you.

> Me. Not nearly as much as I'm missing you.

> R: Is everything okay?

> Me: Yes, everything is okay, but I am still looking for it. I've had no luck today. I really wish I could see you right now.

> R: Do not stress yourself. If plan A doesn't work, then Plan B will. Can you sneak away tomorrow?

Tomorrow wasn't good because I needed to go by Pam's and email some stuff to my attorney. I hated doing too much at home where Elijah may discover it.

This whole situation was so upsetting. Sneaking around meant I had to double and triple check every step I made.

I'd even had to store my love's name under the first letter only, just in case someone saw my screen during an incoming call. I couldn't wait for all of this to be over so that I could rest in the arms of the man I loved.

The phone dinged in my hand again.

> R: Bree, all of this sneaking around will be over soon, so don't worry. If not tomorrow, I know I will see you on Monday. I love you more than anything. You know that, right?

I smiled. I couldn't help it. He knew me so well. Time and time again, he had proven how much he cared about and wanted to protect me.

> Me: Yes, I know and I love you, too.

> R: Good. Call me when you can.

I put the phone down and looked up at Gianna. Her eyes were glued to me and she was grinning from ear to ear.

"Was that lover boy?" she asked.

"Maybe," I replied.

"Are you going to tell me who he is?"

I gave her a look.

Respect and gratitude were an understatement for how I felt about Gianna, but I'd been burned enough, and sharing too much could be dangerous for both of us.

"I'll take that as a no," she said. "But you're happy, right? Whoever this guy is. Whatever the two of you have going on, he makes you happy?"

I touched my hand to my chest. "More than you know."

"Alright," Gianna said, getting to her feet. "I'm going to grab a snack and some uninterrupted TV time while we wait for Pam. I need some more happiness in my life."

Gianna left, and I decided to also use this time to do something that made me happy. Call Ryan.

Picking up my phone, I tucked myself between a tall storage unit and the wall, a common place where my kids hid.

This call had to be done in private because not only was Ryan the man I was having an affair with, he was my husband's best friend.

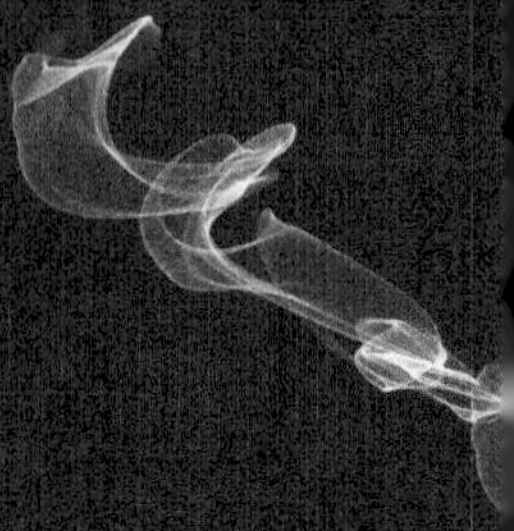

Day 2

SUNDAY
7:30 AM

The dial on the scale spun back and forth for several seconds, working hard to decide how judgmental it wanted to be.

I had those three tacos for dinner last night, but I skipped the sour cream.

Surely that earned me something.

I narrowed my eyes at it and the line settled at a spot somewhere between 142 and 143.

Okay, not so bad.

I released my breath, and it jumped up to 145.

What the hell?!

It was definitely time to switch from the analog to the digital, but I was old-fashioned and loved vintage things. Televisions with the knobs, 1960s style phones with rotary dials, floral wallpaper... yup, I had issues.

Not to mention, my love for traditional things didn't end at decor. It carried on into my marriage. Vows meant something to me, and I had this delusional idea that my marriage could, and would, last forever.

Which is why at one point come hell or high water, I fought to remain with my husband. I refused to let my marriage fall, not realizing that it takes both people to keep a commitment alive. I couldn't keep someone that didn't want to be kept.

And now, my way of thinking had changed. It was time for an upgrade, including wardrobe, decor and spouse.

Soon. Very soon.

"Are you staring at that scale again?" Elijah asked. "I told you, the numbers won't magically fix themselves. You've got to go to the gym."

Elijah was sitting up in bed, with his eyes glued to his work tablet. He was only wearing his boxer briefs and socks, and I had to admit he was still very attractive.

Even in his mid-thirties, the football player's body he sported in college had remained intact and his good looks hadn't faded a bit. Unfortunately for me, neither had his arrogance.

I closed my eyes and swallowed my snappy response.

"It's no big deal," I said in a chipper tone. "I'm only around ten pounds heavier than college. I will keep on with my healthy meals and at home work out videos."

Elijah put his tablet down.

"Fat is fat, Bree. Don't sugarcoat it. Besides, you don't see me needing to adjust my belt size. Change starts in the mind."

I said nothing, but my eyes dropped to the floor, and my shoulders slumped in defeat.

"Come on, don't be like that. I'm just trying to help you out. Make time for yourself. Stick to the goal. Live your vision."

He was coaching me like I was one of his damn athletes.

I gave him a weak smile, folded my arms protectively across my body and spoke in a voice slightly above a whisper.

Intimidated woman activated.

"I know. It's just hard to make time for myself. There is always so much to do around the house and with the kids. I thought I was doing a pretty good job."

"Pretty good isn't good enough," he mumbled under his breath.

Then, noticing me still standing, he sighed and reached out a hand, coaxing me into the bed. Which meant he wanted sex.

Elijah's affection came at a price. Uplifting me, encouraging me or even showing the slightest bit of interest these days meant he wanted something. Since it was 7am on a Sunday morning. I would bet that something was sex.

I placed one knee on the bed and got in. The damn thing had the nerve to creak at the added weight, as if I wasn't taking enough shit from my husband.

I remember when we used to wake up early on the weekends, before the kids to spend time together. We would talk about our days, our plans, and how much we wanted to see and do in life together.

I don't know if my recollection is off, or if I had over romanticized it, but I thought we were happy. It was something I looked forward to.

Now I was grateful when I woke up and he was gone.

"You see, Bree, that's the thing. Sarah has had four kids, and she looks immaculate. If she did it, I know you can."

Was this man still talking shit to me about my weight!?

Sarah was his assistant and the first woman I caught him cheating on me with. Expectantly, I was livid, but I also had my marriage and Zoey, five at the time, to consider.

Elijah apologized and promised that it would never happen again, but of course, it did. With a mortgage broker, a salon owner, a mom from Zoey's school, then again with... actually, I lost track. At this point, it was community dick.

Anyway, it was ballsy for him to bring her up, especially since he still worked with Sarah. But if I started an argument about it, he would do what he always did, flip the tables on me...

"Bree, I made a mistake. Are we seriously going to keep living in the past? Plus, Sarah works for me. We have a professional relationship. Am I simply supposed to ignore her and risk jeopardizing my career over your insecurities?"

I took Elijah's hand in mine and squeezed a little too tight, wishing it was another part of his body I could apply dangerous pressure to. However, he didn't seem to notice.

"I'll keep that in mind, honey," I replied.

Elijah smiled, satisfied that I wasn't pressing the issue any further.

"You know what I want?" He said.

Shaking my head, I pretended not to know.

"The kids aren't up yet and a nice long blowjob would be a perfect way to start my day."

My eyes shifted towards the door. "Are you sure? They might be up any minute."

In a very smooth attempt to win me over, Elijah pulled me on top of him, flattened my chest to his, then squeezed my ass.

"Come on, live a little. I'll make sure I'm quick."

There was a pause on my end as I battled internally before giving in.

"You know what?" I whispered with a grin. "There is something I wanted to try, and now would be the perfect time."

Elijah released me and placed his hands behind his head.

"Alright, then. Let's have it."

I got out of bed and held up one finger. "I'll be right back."

Slipping out the door, I headed to the kitchen, the cool tiled floor chilling my bare feet as I crept to the fridge.

All the while, I silently prayed that Grayson or Ariel didn't wake up. If they did, they would seek me out immediately.

Zoey, on the other hand, would remain in her room until I found a way to convince her to come out.

I'd been waiting three weeks for Elijah to show interest in me. I needed this opportunity.

Opening the fridge, I grabbed a medium-sized grapefruit and made quick work of cutting a hole in the center. I was moving so fast I almost cut myself, but survived unscathed.

When I was done, I made a circle with my thumb and pointer finger, and placed it over the hole.

Yes!

I'd jacked Elijah off enough times over the course of our marriage that my hands had developed muscle memory as it pertained to his size. The cut was a perfect fit!

I held the grapefruit at eye-level and peered straight through. It wouldn't be deep enough to cover his entire penis, but if everything went smoothly, it wouldn't need to be.

Note to self: Try this with Ryan.

After cleaning up the mess from the grapefruit, I put the knife in the dishwasher and went upstairs to surprise my awaiting husband.

Elijah immediately sat up when he saw what I was holding.

This had been a dream of his ever since, Matteo, Gianna's husband, let it slip that she used a grapefruit on him during oral and how amazing it felt.

In response, Elijah commented I was "Too boring to do anything so kinky" and I never forgot how left out that must have made him feel.

My poor husband simply wanted in on the fun, and today, he could have it all.

"Are you going to do what I think you are?" he asked excitedly.

I nodded.

Elijah needed no further response or persuading. Yanking down his boxers, he tossed them to the floor and relaxed back onto the pillow.

Positioning myself between his legs, I said, "You just sit back. I got this."

Placing the grapefruit carefully over his dick, I pulled it down inch by inch until the head popped through. Then I grabbed a small bottle of lotion from my nightstand and squeezed some into my hand.

"What's that for?" Elijah asked, confused. "Aren't you going to use your mouth?"

"Trust me, it will feel better this way, I promise."

Sliding my hand over the top of his dick, I massaged it with the lotion.

Elijah moaned with pleasure, and I took that as my cue to begin. The whole time I fought hard to not think about all the women he'd been inside and pretended to enjoy it.

After a few seconds, I stopped stroking him and let the grapefruit do most of the work, as I glided it up and down, coating his dick with the sticky citrus juice.

"Yes, Bree! That feels so good!"

The juice continuously oozed out, and I pumped his erection faster and harder, thanking God that the task, at my literal hand, would be over soon.

True to his word, for once, Elijah came quick, jerking and gripping the covers as his cum coated the top of the unlucky grapefruit.

I lifted it free and his dick fell limply to the side. The left side, to be exact. It, too, was predictable.

"That... was... amazing," he huffed.

I smiled and gave him a quick peck on the cheek. Then, getting up from the bed, I carefully balanced the fruit so that none of his cum dripped over the sides and headed toward the door.

"I'll go discard this and get breakfast started."

It took him a moment, but he finally said, "I'll take my usual."

"Sure thing," I replied over my shoulder, turning the knob.

Back in the kitchen, I placed the grapefruit on the counter and collected all the items needed for Elijah's breakfast smoothie.

As I add each item to the blender, the cruelty of what I was about to do forced me to recall a rather unforgettable experience from grade school.

One cup of almond milk.

When I was in second grade, my teacher, Mrs. Bland, took us to the principal's office one Thursday morning to watch a snake eat a mouse. All the kids, especially the boys, thought it was so cool, but I didn't share their sentiments.

It was disgusting, cruel and a little barbaric for seven-year-olds, if you ask me.

Half a cup of strawberries and three blueberries.

In went the tiny white mouse, with its red beady eyes deep down into the giant glass tank. It seemed calm in the beginning, exploring its new environment with fascination and joy. Little did he know it was time for the show to begin.

One banana

The snake perked up, realizing that there was something in its midst that wasn't there moments before. Unfortunately, the mouse senses it too, a looming darkness that it can't avoid.

Now, defenseless and terrified, the mouse rushes to the corner of the tank and huddles, shaking, scratching, desperately seeking a way out.

1 tablespoon of almond butter

But the mouse doesn't make it. He isn't smart enough, fast enough or lucky enough to survive the predator and I watch him, with my innocent seven-year-old eyes, vanish from sight.

One-quarter cup of Greek yogurt.

But why did the mouse have to die? Wasn't there some

artificial food that big slimy snake could have gulped up instead? I didn't understand then, but I do now.

Those that can't fight back fall to the bottom of the food chain, where the snakes of the world will devour you.

Half a cup of baby spinach.

I think of that mouse often. Replaying the unfair treatment, the look of panic in its eyes, and the torturous death. I wish I could turn back the hands of time and stand up for him.

Picking up the grapefruit, I tilt it ever so slightly and watch Elijah's semen drizzle into the plastic cylinder, covering a leaf of spinach. Placing the lid on the blender, I press the start button and watch it go.

This one's for you, mouse.

8:30 AM

"This smoothie tastes weird. Did you add something different?"

It should taste different. You are essentially drinking a dose of your own medicine.

I paused from feeding Ariel. The spoonful of oatmeal hovered in midair and I gave Elijah my full attention.

"No, I can't think of..." I snapped my fingers, with the hand not holding the spoon. "Your usual almond milk wasn't available, so I had to pick up an off brand. I'm sorry. Does it taste bad?"

Elijah frowned at the cup. "It's a little bitter." He took another sip and then shrugged. "I guess I can handle it. But next time, tell me in advance. I don't like surprises."

I nodded and gave him another apologetic look.

Turning to Ariel, my attention was once again interrupted when Grayson, sitting next to me, said, "Mom, can I hang out at Keith's today after I finish practicing my soccer with dad?"

"That's a question I can't answer. Why don't you—" I was going to direct Grayson to ask his dad, when Elijah cut me off.

"No can do today, buddy. I've got work."

Elijah drank the last of his smoothie, dropped the cup into the sink, and walked over to the table. He was already dressed for work, and moving something around in his pocket. It must have been his cellphone, buzzing. It was always buzzing.

My heart broke for Grayson.

I'm certain my asshole of a husband was about to let him down, again. He has only fulfilled his promise of playing soccer with Grayson twice since he joined the team last year.

Ariel must have sensed that this was going to take a while, because she pulled the spoon from my hand.

I let her take it.

She could very well feed herself. The problem was she had a tendency to get more on the floor than in her mouth. Feeding her myself was faster and cleaner.

"But dad," Grayson whined, looking up at Elijah. "You said you would help me practice my control move."

Elijah laid a hand on Grayson's shoulder.

"I know that's what I said, but I have no control over when my clients need me. You must learn to be a big boy sometimes. There is always next weekend."

"That's what you say all the time," Grayson said, biting off a piece of bacon.

Elijah gave me a "you can jump in at anytime," glare.

I ignored him and turned my attention toward Zoey. The only greeting she'd given me before pulling up a chair and putting her earbuds in was, "Hey."

What happened to the little girl that gave me hugs and kisses, simply because? Who needed me to keep the monsters away at night? And kiss away any boo-boos she had?

The girl that sat before me hardly spoke to me anymore and trying to get her to talk made things worse.

Vaguely, I heard Elijah respond to Grayson with yet another excuse and the two went back and forth as I fought the rising guilt.

Amid all the chaos and complexity, my primary concern was to ensure that my children did not endure any further hardship. That was becoming harder and harder and might only worsen once Elijah and I split.

"That's Final Grayson!" Elijah shouted, storming out of the kitchen.

Ariel, Zoey, and I watched him go.

Grayson's eyes were downcast, but I could see tears drop onto his plate.

My poor baby.

I leaned close, rested my chin on his shoulder and said, "After breakfast, you can go to Keith's and you two can practice. Then, the next time daddy is free, you can show him your new moves."

Grayson slowly looked up and gave me a weak smile. "Thanks, mom."

"Bree, a word, please." Elijah called from the living room.

I gave Grayson a kiss on the cheek and stood. Zoey and Ariel were already back to minding their own business.

Zoey was listening to a song so loud that it almost blew out my eardrums, and Ariel was coating the floor beneath her with sticky oats.

"Why didn't you say anything?" Elijah asked, turning on me as soon as I set foot inside the spacious room.

I crossed my arms and frowned at him. "What did you want me to say? He misses you, Elijah, and wants to be with you."

"Oh, so now I'm the bad guy? I want to spend time with

him too, but bills don't pay themselves. He is going to have to understand that I can't be at his beck and call."

"He doesn't think that."

"Maybe he wouldn't if you would back me up. You left me out in the cold."

I threw up my hands in surrender. "Grayson needed to speak to you, not to me. You are his dad. Don't make me run interference."

"Stop reminding me that I am his dad, as if I don't know it. And no one is asking you to run interference. I want you to do a mother's job and keep the kids under control."

"The kids *are* under control," I retorted angrily, working diligently to keep my voice down.

"Grayson sure isn't. He is harassing me about practicing when you know I don't have the time. Plus, I keep catching him outside my office door and sometimes he simply walks in! No knocking or anything, like he owns the place."

"Once again," I said in an obvious tone, "he's only looking for time with his dad."

"Yeah, whatever," Elijah spat, then turned away from me. "It's called manners. How about you teach him some?"

He walked toward the couch and that's when I noticed the small box that was sitting there. Poking out from the top were a signed football jersey and a few high school trophies.

Elijah picked it up and faced my direction again, but he didn't make eye contact with me.

"What's that?" I asked.

"Just some stuff I am taking by the office for the guys to see. No biggie."

That was an entire lie.

Elijah was taking that box to his condo. The one that I learned per yet another recording that he rented a few months ago.

He'd been taking out small boxes of stuff here and there, but slowly, in order to not raise suspicions.

"Anyway, I have to go," he said, walking past me. "Don't wait up for me tonight. Going to be busy with clients, then meeting some friends."

Likely, one of those friends would be Ryan.

My Ryan.

I'd love to see him. The last time I did, we fucked like rabbits and I came twice. He was much better in bed than Elijah.

Oh, wait, it was Sunday.

Elijah wouldn't be with Ryan because Ryan would be at Val's Sports Bar.

Every Sunday, throughout the entire football season, that is where Ryan watched the football game.

It was a ritual he started five years ago when his dad was alive, but now he still went alone. I didn't want to impose on the loving memory he had with his dad. So unfortunately, I'd have to catch up with him tomorrow.

After breakfast, I dropped Grayson off at Keiths, Zoey at the mall, and Ariel with my parents.

Now, home alone. I could finally get the recorder set back up in Elijah's office before I needed to go to Pam's.

Once I jimmied the lock for a frustrating few minutes, I finally got it open and went inside.

I put the recorder in its usual hiding spot, tucked safely behind a bare English Ivy plant that sat in the corner, but before activating it, I stood in front of Elijah's desk and surveyed the office.

Several times, I'd searched every inch of this room and found nothing. There was still the outdoor shed and attic left to search, but if it wasn't there, I was at a loss.

Leaning forward, I shook the mouse, and the desktop came to life. Typing in the password that I'd known for years, I did my familiar steps of checking his email, digging into the recently deleted trash, and various other things that could build my case.

In the end, I found nothing concerning the deal or the whereabouts of my software. Everything on this computer was work related and not the least bit incriminating.

I bet all the juicy stuff was on his laptop.

No major loss, though. Thanks to my knack for planting evidence, I'd made a substantial leap in building my divorce case and messaging his mistress was going to be a big help.

I was out of there in twenty minutes, locking the office behind me and heading to my car.

"Hi, Bree!" my neighbor Hilary shouted just as I was opening my car door.

My plan was to ignore her, but being Hilary, she didn't give up so easily.

"Bree, oh Bree," she called out.

I turned to face her and wasn't the least bit surprised. Hilary was wearing a purple leotard, over fitted black leggings, her hair up into a bun and her smile as bright as the morning sun.

She was a ballerina teacher who had a reputation for promoting her body before her brain and was always up to no good.

"I only wanted to say hello. I hope you and Elijah have a good day."

Adjusting the black bag that hung on my shoulder, I looked left, right, got up on tiptoes and even did a full circle for dramatic effect.

"Do you see Elijah with me?!" I snapped.

Hilary placed a hand on her cheek and squatted slightly to get a better look inside my car.

"Oh, my mistake, dear. I thought he was already in the car, toodle-oo."

I watched Hilary saunter her slimy ass all the way back into her house, while thinking, I'd like to toodle her fucking oo and then I'd take that stupid bun she always wore and beat her ass with that, too.

Hilary was fake and obnoxious.

A well-known home wrecker in the neighborhood that none of the wives trusted. I'm not one for jumping on bandwagons, but I had to agree with them.

Ms. Ballet wasn't pulling the wool over my eyes.

I knew exactly what she was up to. Therefore, before I lost my cool and did something I would regret, I forced myself to jump in the car and go handle my business.

Five minutes into the drive to Pam's, I had forgotten all about Hilary, moving on to bigger things.

The quiet drive gave me time to rack my brain and, as a result, increased my anxiety. I only had fourteen days left and never assumed I'd be cutting it this close.

If I didn't find what I needed in the next few days, my perfect plan would be weakened immensely.

Pulling into Pam's driveway, her Labrador, Rain, instantly greeted me.

"Hey boy!" I said, giving him the rubbing affection he sought.

"Can I at least get my hug in before you start drooling all over her?" Pam said, approaching, playfully nudging Rain aside.

Pam hugged me tight, and I breathed in her familiar scent of rose and honey. She was like a sister to me and having known Elijah for just as long as I did; it felt like she understood me more than anyone.

"How are you?" she asked, taking a step back.

Her eyes were empathetic and warm. The question was simple, but the answer was heavy.

"Could be better," I admitted, then tapped the bag on my

shoulder. "Got more evidence to forward to my lawyer, so I'll need your computer. But I'm still standing."

"Sounds like someone could use a drink," Pam said, tossing an arm around my shoulder and leading me to the deck.

"It's going to take more than one," I replied with a laugh.

Rain followed us to the backyard, immediately getting lost when he spotted a squirrel near the fence.

Pam already had the table set with wine, chips, dip and, most importantly, her laptop, so I took a seat on the long wicker couch with an orange cushion.

I had a computer at home, but I didn't like to use it when sending things to my lawyer. Elijah wasn't a snooper, but I could never be too sure.

Therefore, once a week I came over to Pams and she let me use her laptop to handle all of my business. Usually while she ran errands, played with Rain, or cleaned.

Pam poured us both a glass of red wine and we enjoyed a few sips before speaking.

"I still can't believe Elijah is doing this to you. It seems like just yesterday the four of us were in college, planning our lives without a care in the world. You two were so in love and now you are practically enemies."

The four of us that Pam was referring to included her, myself, Elijah and Ryan.

During those days, we were all pretty much inseparable. Cramming for exams together, visiting one another's family during breaks and spending Friday night at Johnny's Pizza on campus, because a large pepperoni between the four of us was all we could afford.

It was a great experience with even better memories, but at present, we had morphed into something entirely different. Greed, temptation, jealousy and lousy luck had divided us all in one way or another.

I took another sip, realized it was not even close to enough to numb me, then finished the glass.

"Elijah is who he has always been," I said. "He loves according to convenience and necessity, and I am no longer necessary."

"That's not true."

"You can lie to yourself, but now that I think about it. Elijah was only with me because I was a nerd."

Pam shook her head and the wine in her glass sloshed so close to the rim that some spilled out.

"You were not a nerd! Who cares that you helped him on a few tests and wrote a few papers? We all helped each other back then."

I held up a finger.

"No, I wrote *all* of his papers and helped him cheat on *most* of his tests. Face it. I was so happy a popular jock liked me I was blind to anything else. I am sure he only stayed after college because we had Zoey."

Pam swatted at a fly darting back and forth until it lost interest and said, "Well, I think he did love you. He was a good guy back then and maybe now he has simply lost his way."

"He's lost his mind," I said, refilling the wine glass. "Next subject please."

Pam frowned and then her expression turned cheerful. "I made some stuffed peppers, jasmine rice and banana bread. Do you want me to send you home with a few plates?"

My mouth watered at the mere mention of Pam's cooking. She was the best cook I knew and anytime I could skip making dinner felt like winning the lottery.

"Hell yeah I do," I replied, then narrowed my eyes at her. Pam only cooked when she was stressed. "What's going on?"

Pam fidgeted with a thread on her skirt and chewed her bottom lip. "Nothing."

"You had a late shift yesterday, came over to help me, and

then you were supposed to come home and get some rest. Let me guess, you didn't get the rest?"

"Fine! I am thinking about giving Dylan another chance, okay?"

My mouth fell open, but I shut it quickly when the fly from earlier came to mind.

I loved Pam, but she made the dumbest choices when it came to men. Every guy she fell for was always a cheater, abuser, or both.

The woman was drawn to them like a moth to a flame and they burned her ass every single time.

"Pam, he has cheated on you five times! And the last time he left, he stole your rent money!"

Pam buried her face in her hands.

"I know," she sighed, shaking her head.

"Obviously you don't," I nearly shouted. "And what about the woman he left you for? Isn't he still with her?"

"Yeah, but he said he will leave her if I take him back," Pam said, her face still hidden by her hands.

Is this what I sounded like all these years with Elijah? A pathetic mess

"That makes no sense, Pam. If he wants to leave her, then he will. You taking him back will not be a factor. Sounds to me like he is still playing you."

"But," I heard her say in a quiet voice, "maybe he's changed?"

It was a question.

A question that she expected me to answer because she was now peeking up at me like a kid afraid of being reprimanded.

It made me wonder, *was this unfortunate ability to not only fall in love, but to remain with disloyal men, simply part of our family DNA?*

My mom was still with my dad, and he had cheated. I

stayed with Elijah all these years and he never deserved me, and poor Pam, although single, was living an identical life.

I gave her the same pitying smile she had given me when I arrived and then took her hand.

"No, Pam, he hasn't changed, and if you don't stop this insanity you call a dating life, it is going to land you somewhere you don't want to be. Women that get burned may want retribution."

Fear filled her eyes. The thought had never dawned on her that the other woman might not quietly fade into the background.

"Wait! You think the girl he's with might try to get back at me in some way?"

I shrugged. "You can never be sure. Cheating is messy, and Dylan likes the mayhem. Which is why he left you for her in the first place. Remember the guy you wouldn't help him rob?"

"Yeah," she said slowly, "but stop calling it that. The guy owed him money. Dylan was only taking back what was his and needed someone to help him get into the guy's apartment."

Was she really this dense about men?

"Alright," I said, crossing my arms. "If it were no big deal. Why didn't you help him?"

Now my cousin seemed even more conflicted. Her shoulders dropped, and I heard a light cracking in the wicker as she shifted in the chair.

Evidently, she hadn't thought about any of this.

I shook my head. No, I couldn't and wouldn't be that stupid.

Maybe in the past I was, but never again. Watching Pam's eyes dart back and forth filled with emotions of denial and uncertainty made my next steps crystal clear.

Opening my black leather bag, I pulled out two folders

and a USB drive. Picking up the computer, I placed it in my lap and looked over at the woman that deserved more pity than me.

"I'm going to get started sending this stuff to my lawyers. Shouldn't take me long. We can go get our nails done after if you want."

"Sure," Pam murmured. She grabbed her wineglass and patted me on the shoulder. "Alright, I'll leave you to it. Rain has an appointment with the groomers. I should be back in a few hours."

I watched her go, with only one thought on my mind as I logged in.

Elijah, you asshole, payback is gonna be a bitch.

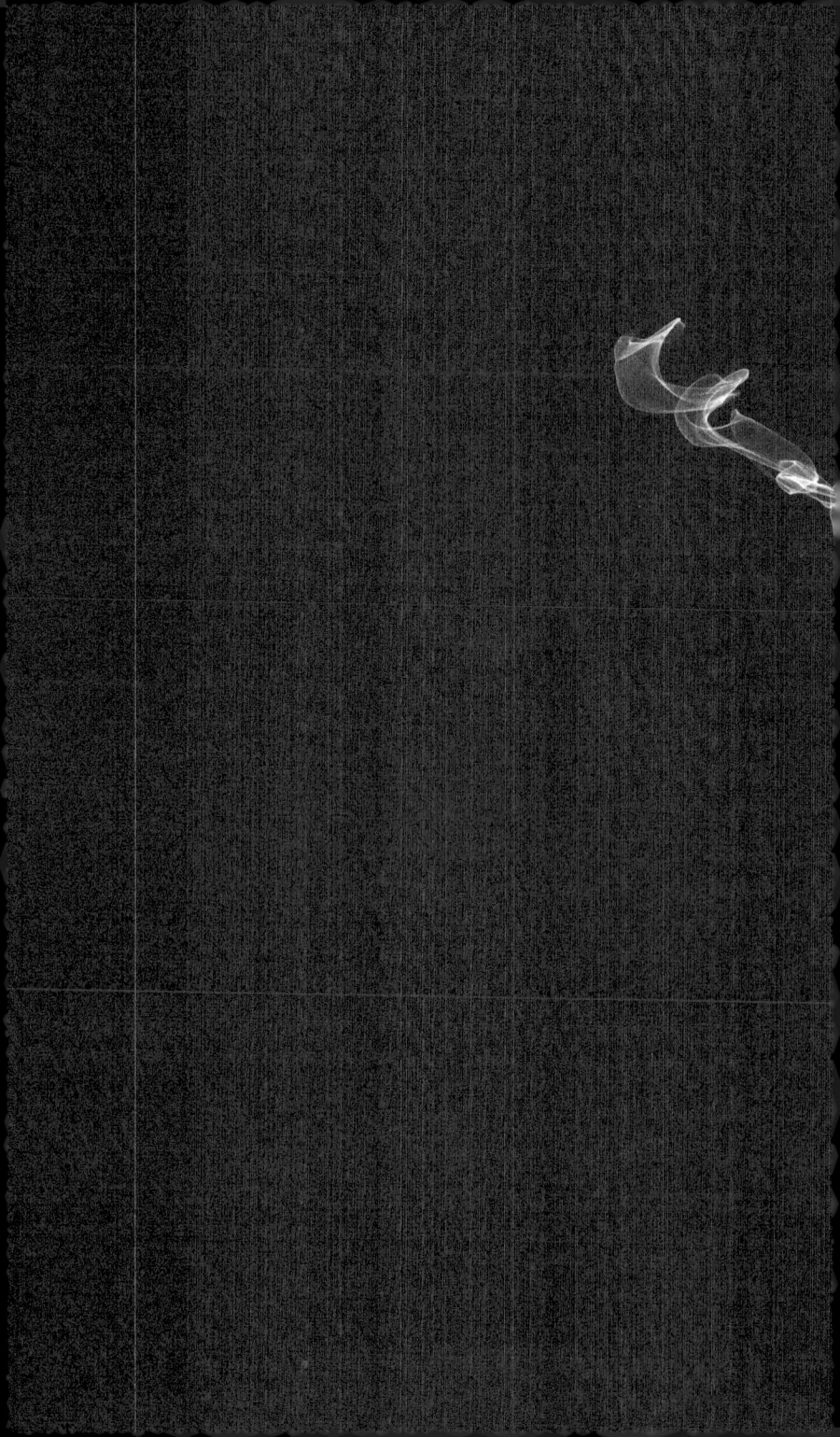

Day 3

MONDAY
11:45 AM

Ariel pressed the elevator button again and again before the door eventually opened. I'd told her many times that it doesn't make it arrive any faster, but I won't today because I've learned my lesson.

In the past, I always found myself in a debate with a three-year-old and since they don't subscribe to a higher level of logic, it was always me who lost a few brain cells.

Never again.

Wasting no time in her pink and yellow tutu and white and red t-shirt that said "daddy's girl", Ariel rushed inside the elevator and continued to be a hyperactive ball of energy.

Watching her dart from one side of the elevator to the other reminded me of a blur of flashing lights that threatened to invoke a seizure.

We visited Elijah at work at least once a month to have lunch with him, and my daughter lived for these visits. Likely because the entire office spoiled her.

"Are you excited to see daddy?" I asked.

"Yes, I am," she said in that adorable voice that made me give her one extra cookie, even though I'd said no more.

"Mama E!" Ariel shouted, running towards the receptionist area as soon as we exited the elevator.

Evelyn, whom everyone in the building referenced as

Mama E, was a sweet, lively woman in her 60s that handled the front desk for Red Zone Sports Agency.

"Is that my sweet baby?" Evelyn said, coming around the desk.

She lifted Ariel into her arms and twirled her around before giving her a big kiss on the cheek. Ariel responded by wrapping her arms around the woman's neck and giving her a tight hug.

Evelyn coughed. "Not too tight, sweetie. Mama E's lungs aren't as strong as they used to be."

We both laughed, and she set Ariel down on the floor.

"Hi Bree," Evelyn said, hugging me as well. "Back for the monthly lunch?"

"Yup," I said, lifting the giant bag of food that I was carrying. "Today we are having spaghetti."

Evelyn gave me a knowing look over her wire-rimmed glasses. "In that dress, I think Elijah is going to want more than spaghetti."

I feigned shock and then laughed at her comment. It wasn't as if I hadn't worn this dress to get attention.

It was a stunning shade of blue with subtle hints of gold, and it embraced my body in a way that highlighted my best features. I didn't think Elijah would appreciate it, but Ryan sure would.

Ariel and I were about to head towards Elijah's office when Evelyn said, "Oh wait, I have something for you, little princess."

Within seconds, she retrieved a small teddy bear from her desk.

"I saw this at the store this weekend and couldn't resist."

Ariel squealed with delight, hugged Evelyn again, and we walked the short distance to Elijah's office.

The only thing was it took us fifteen minutes to get there,

because we, or rather Ariel, kept stopping to socialize and receive compliments on how pretty her outfit was.'

And at every stop, she would spin around several billion times, modeling it for them, usually receiving a gift in the process.

At Tom's desk, Ariel was gifted a shiny ink pen. At Jane's, two pieces of candy and when she was done playing a 2 minute game of tag with Gary, she received a whole $5 to go toward her college fund.

I must say, these visits had turned quite lucrative for my little three-year-old.

When we finally arrived at Elijah's office, I was pleasantly surprised to also find Ryan.

He was sitting in front of Elijah's desk, pointing at numbers on a page in an open folder.

Immediately, I recognized the image of the popular sports professional in the upper left-hand corner of the page. I'd seen him on several commercials promoting healthy snacks and high protein bars, however for the life of me I couldn't remember his name.

"Daddy!"

Before he could stand, Ariel ran around the desk and hugged him.

I deposited my purse and the bag containing our lunch onto a small glass table near the door, then turned to watch them. Elijah pulled her up onto his knee and bounced Ariel a few times, causing her to erupt into giggles.

"How's my girl?" Elijah asked.

Instead of answering the question, Ariel shoved the bear in his face. "Look what Mama E got for me."

As soon as Elijah took it, Ariel turned her attention to his keyboard and hit several keys.

"What does this button do?" she asked. "Or this one?" she said, hitting another.

Elijah struggled to slow her down, explaining the importance of not touching his computer, but it backfired because now she was hitting the button on his desk phone.

I didn't care.

I was discreetly watching Ryan, and he was watching me. The greeting between us needed to be casual, which was why I didn't rush into his arms immediately.

"Bree," Ryan said, standing to embrace me. "You having a good day?"

"Yes, thank you for asking. What about you?"

"We booked Calvin Sombers," he said, nodding towards the folder on the desk, "so I can't complain."

Oh, that's right!

Sombers was the football player that owned, Balanced Act, a business geared towards providing personal trainers for athletes. Ryan told me he was trying to score him as a client last month, but the conversation was cut short because we decided to do our own workout plan in his bedroom.

Elijah, who was now fed up with Ariel's wandering hands, set her down and instructed her to go back to me. However, she ignored that directive and went straight to Ryan, tugging on his pants leg.

Ryan's eyes shifted from me downward to Ariel. "And how are you... Daddy's girl?" He said, reading the shirt.

"I'm good. Can I have a..." she thought about it "Cor...tar?"

He crouched down to get eye level with her. "Hmm, that depends. Maybe I will give you a quarter," he said, pronouncing the word correctly, "but what do you need it for?"

"Candy, silly," Ariel replied enthusiastically.

"Have you been a good girl?"

"Yes," she said, looking up at me for approval.

Don't try it, kid. I'm not lying to support your habits.

Ryan lifted Ariel high into the air and her tiny hands instantly cupped his handsome face.

Elijah, oblivious to this entire exchange, sat at his desk, taken in by something on his computer screen.

"Tell you what," Ryan said. "I will give you two quarters if you can sing me the alphabet."

Never the shy one, Ariel began belting out her alphabets.

"A.B.C.D..."

Several people walking by Elijah's office stopped to hear the show. The girl even got a round of applause and additional quarters.

Hell, maybe I should sing the alphabet.

After giving Ariel a high five, Ryan returned to his office, leaving Elijah, the singer, and me to our family lunch time.

Ariel pulled her iPad from my purse and sat in her favorite spot on the floor. I grabbed the lunch bag, sat it down on Elijah's desk and waited.

Still, fixated with something on his screen, he didn't even notice me.

I wanted desperately to see what it was because I truly needed something to point me in the direction of my fucking software!

I refused to go forward with the rest of my plan without it.

My husband finally looked up at me, taking several seconds for his eyes to focus.

"Bree! I almost forgot you were here. What did you bring for lunch?"

Seriously! That's it? Ungrateful bastard.

"Hi, honey... My day was well... Aww, I'm happy to see you, too," I said, engaging in an imaginary conversation that included the common decency I wish he'd shown.

Elijah gritted his teeth. "Don't start. After the morning I had I am not in the mood. I already know you had a good day.

You seem fine. Ariel is happy, and I'm starving. Can you just tell me what's for lunch?"

"Fine," I grumbled, opening the bag.

Taking out three covered bowls, I lined them up on the desk.

One contained spaghetti, the second a salad, and the third belonged to Ariel. It was her chicken nuggets and tater tots.

Elijah picked up the bowl of spaghetti and removed the lid.

"Mmm, your famous spaghetti. I can't wait to dig in."

"Well, you will have to wait," I said, taking it from his hands. "I need to warm this and Ariel's food up first. Watch her for me while I go to the break room, okay?"

"Sure," he responded, attention already back on the computer screen.

I glanced at Ariel, who was currently consumed by magical castles, princesses and toads singing on her screen. She would be fine.

At the end of the hallway, I made a left turn instead of a right one, walking opposite of the break room.

My presence in this hallway wouldn't raise suspicions, but if I didn't stay vigilant, I could find myself drawn into unwanted conversations about Ariel or my personal life.

Once I arrived in front of the office door, I knocked lightly before going in.

Ryan looked up and grinned, dropping the file that was in his hand. Papers slipped out of it onto his desk, but he paid it no mind, already coming toward me.

"You always make me wait so long."

"That's because you are an impatient man," I said, locking the door.

"Only when it concerns you."

He took the bowls from my hand and put them on a glass

table, identical to the one in Elijah's office, before kissing me deeply.

This was what I desired, what I was looking for. The touch and embrace from the man that reminded me why Elijah wasn't worthy of me and deserved every ounce of my wrath.

"Did anyone see you?" Ryan asked.

"No," I said, pulling him back down for another kiss.

It took effort, but eventually we stopped fondling each other, or at least I did, since Ryan's hands were now squeezing my ass.

"You look amazing today," he said. "I love this dress on you."

"Good, because I wore it especially for you. Are you coming over tonight?"

Ryan took his time answering. Choosing to first spin me around and visually drank all of me in.

"Yup. It's Monday night football. I wouldn't miss it. Not to mention the chance to be near you." He tightened his arms around my waist, his eyes boring into mine. "Maybe we can sneak off and..." He stopped talking and lifted a suggestive brow.

"Anything you want," I said, committing to some future erotic play. "The kids will be asleep, and Gianna and her husband will be over. I think that should keep Elijah busy."

We shared one last kiss before reluctantly separating.

I straightened his tie and wiped the lipstick from his lips. Then took a minute to fix my own clothes before grabbing the bowls and going to the actual break room this time.

With absolute joy in my heart, I returned to the office, Ariel and Elijah still where I'd left them.

We hadn't been eating long before another visitor stopped by. This one made Ariel drop her nuggets and abandon her tablet.

At this point, I think she saw everyone in the office as nothing more than peasants whose sole purpose was to bring her gifts.

"Did I hear that the princess was here?" Came the voice of a man peeking his head into the office.

It was Elijah's boss, Victor Grafton.

"BIC - TOR!" Ariel practically screamed, ruining the man's name.

However, he didn't seem to care, especially after she locked her tiny limbs around his leg, just like she had with Ryan.

"Did you bring it? Did you bring it?" She asked, jumping up and down.

"Do I ever break a promise?" he said.

Ariel shook her head emphatically. Her two ponytails slapping against her chubby cheeks.

Revealing what he was holding behind his back caused Ariel's eyes to bulge and all cheerful sounds to cease.

She took the box that contained a train set from Victor's hand and held it up like it was some long-lost treasure.

"Woooowww", she whispered, stretching out the word.

The train set, which included lights, cargo cars, curved tracks, signposts, and decor, was a smaller replica of Victor's five-hundred piece train set that he kept in his office.

Whenever we visited, Ariel spent at least a half an hour playing with it. The last time she was here, Victor promised he would buy her one and have it for her when she returned.

I shook my head in defeat.

Victor was just as bad as everyone else in the office spoiling her rotten.

"Mommy, can I play with it now?"

"No!" Elijah and I said simultaneously.

The fact that he said anything was astonishing, since he'd barely paid us any attention.

But then I realized that Ariel making a mess and playing with a loud toy would make it harder for him to pretend we weren't here, and he couldn't have that.

"When we get home this evening, sweetie. I will set it up for you, but not right now, okay?"

Ariel looked momentarily sad, but then said, "Polly said have patience."

My heart swelled.

Repetition worked, it really worked!

I'd been working on manners for a while and was starting to think I'd have to wash my hands of her. Hey, raising two out of three model citizens wasn't bad.

Eventually I tried a show featuring Polly, the talking parrot, who taught kids about patience, manners and respect.

Dare I think it was working?

We all clapped at Ariel's mature response, and that made her even happier. She gave Victor another hug, told him he was her best friend, and returned to her tablet.

I mouthed a thank you to Victor for giving Ariel yet another reason to smile and then sat down in a chair next to her.

We'd known Victor for twelve years. He'd taken Elijah under his wing and showed him the ropes of the sports industry, making my husband the brilliant and successful agent he now was.

At one point they were close, but nowadays I had no idea what their relationship was like, since Elijah was obviously lying to Victor as well.

It was sad really, because after all Victor had done, how had Elijah thanked him?

Based on the recordings I'd heard, it became evident that Elijah was unable to secure investors for the software eight years ago.

However, this time around, he somehow managed to illegally obtain a confidential list of the original investors in Victor's company, which he was using to build his own sports agency.

My husband's greed knew no bounds.

"Hey, Elijah," Victor said. "Did you have time to make that meeting this morning with the manager from the Saints?"

"No," Elijah said, exhaling in frustration. "Some neighborhood delinquents obviously thought it would be funny to let the air out of my tires and I had to wait for a fucking," he paused and glanced at Ariel, who seemingly hadn't heard a thing. "Tow truck to show up so that I could get the tires fixed."

It was me. I was the delinquent.

I woke up at the crack of dawn, ripped the valves off those bad boys and watched them deflate from the window in the living room, while I enjoyed my morning coffee. The whole thing only took like five to seven minutes.

When Elijah went outside and lost his shit, yelling and screaming about how disrespectful someone had to be to do that, I had a good laugh.

"Whoa, sorry to hear that," Victor said. "Were you able to reschedule?"

"Yeah, for next week."

The guys resumed talking about boring work stuff and I zoned out. I didn't care about Elijah's problems; I had enough of my own.

Where was my damn software?

9:30 PM

"How the hell does he fumble a ball that close to the goal?" Elijah shouted at Matteo.

In his defense, it wasn't Matteo that was igniting his anger, but a running back that obviously had what Ryan and Elijah had referred to for the last half hour as jello hands.

Elijah was drunk and barely standing upright. He stumbled from side to side, pointing at the TV and then shaking his head.

Matteo, Gianna's highly competitive and also currently intoxicated husband, took a long swig of beer before responding. "Because they don't have good fucking trainers, man. I told you this team went to shit ever since they switched out running backs. They should pay us to watch it."

"That's why we wouldn't represent Gordon," Ryan interjected, adding his own perspective. "He is going to be cut from the team before he knows it."

Me and Gianna exchanged a look before going back to enjoying our daiquiris. The guys had taken over the deck with their jumping, yelling and cheering, so she and I sat at a table with two chairs in the corner having our own football party.

The table was adorned with hot wings and all the necessary ingredients to make daiquiris, which meant we didn't have to keep going back and forth to the kitchen.

I'd already had two tonight, but since the kids were asleep and we were outside on the deck, I was free to enjoy a few more.

The weather was absolutely perfect on this beautiful autumn night and I felt alive.

Flipping my glass over, I twisted the rim on a small platter covered in sugar before pouring rum, lime juice and syrup into my glass.

"Look at him," Gianna said with disgust. "Laughing and enjoying himself like his isn't the devil incarnate. Makes me sick."

Elijah was having a good time and usually I, too, was pissed in his presence, but it was hard to be angry with Ryan around. I actually felt giddy. Everything was going to work out.

We even kept stealing glances at one another when we were certain that no one was watching.

"Elijah is being Elijah. Doesn't bother me anymore."

I added the blended frozen strawberries to my glass and tasted it to see if it had enough alcohol. It didn't.

"Have you gone completely wacko on me? Or are you this calm because you found the software?" Gianna whispered. The excitement in her voice was unmistakable.

I glanced over at the guys to ensure they weren't within earshot, but what I noticed was that Ryan had left. The label to his beer was facing me. That was my cue to wait a minute and then meet him inside.

"No, I haven't," I replied, giving Gianna my full attention. "But I'm not worried."

Gianna didn't hide her disappointment. She was still pressuring me to cut my losses and leave, certain that I didn't have enough time left to find anything.

"This entire ordeal is running up my blood pressure." She gulped down the rest of her daiquiri and then picked up the bottle of white rum and downed a giant swig of it as well. "I mean, fuck! I feel like I live on the edge of my seat. If I have to increase the dosage on my blood pressure meds, I am sending the bill straight to you."

"And I will gladly pay it," I announced, seizing the bottle from her hand and taking my own big gulp.

I was supposed to meet Ryan in a second, but I was contemplating sneaking a cigarette and going into the garage instead.

I know I'd just told Gianna that Elijah didn't bother me, but the truth was his mere existence was threatening to ruin my mood. He was now across the way, telling Matteo what a dedicated father he was.

Placing the bottle of rum back on the table, which was pointless because Gianna picked it up again, I stood and glanced down at her.

"I am going to check on the kids. Do you need me to bring anything back?"

"The software would be nice," she said with a smirk.

"Fuck you, too," I said with a grin and walked away.

I entered the house and looked around. All was quiet. Which meant the kids were sound asleep and momma could have some fun.

I knew Ryan was waiting for me in the downstairs bathroom, so quietly, I made my way through the dark kitchen and tiptoed down the short hallway.

Turning the knob, I stuck my head inside and there he was, posted up against the wall, head tilted back. He immediately stood when he saw me.

"There you are," he said, rushing to wrap his arms around me. "I was tempted to come out there and get you. Screw getting caught."

With a grin I said, "Well, I'm here now, so what would you like to do about it?"

Ryan wasted no time.

He lifted me onto the countertop and worked my jeans and underwear over my ass, down my thighs, and to my ankles. In my urgency to assist him, I knocked over the hand soap dispenser.

It rolled to the edge of the counter and landed on the floor.

Thank God it was plastic.

He kneeled down in front of me, yanked me towards the edge, and shoved my thighs apart. His head was between my legs within seconds, hungrily sucking, licking and kissing all of my annoyances from mere minutes ago away.

As Ryan worked his magic, and I held on to his head for

dear life, grinding against his face and concentrating to keep my moans low. Ryan had always been great at anything sexual.

When we were in college, he had gotten a reputation for being a ladies' man. It was the one reason I had more interest in Elijah than him. They may have been friends, but at the time, Elijah was more reserved.

If I had known better, I would have saved myself some sanity and gone directly to Ryan.

One hand gripped the edge of the countertop, and the other I planted firmly against the wall, using it to brace myself for the building release that I knew was soon to come.

"Bree?"

Elijah's voice jolted me from my moment of ecstasy.

It sounded like he was right on the other side of the door!

Ryan immediately stopped licking me into oblivion and his eyes darted up to mine, the same "Oh shit" expression displayed on both of our faces.

My attention shifted to the doorknob, and my stomach tightened. I had forgotten to lock the door!

Moving in what seemed like slow motion, I did the only thing I could think of and hit the light switch.

The bathroom became immersed in total darkness, a millisecond before Elijah opened the door.

"Bree?" He said, stating my name more like a question. "Are you in here?"

The small glow of the hallway plugin light made one side of his face somewhat visible, but the other half was concealed in a dark shadow.

"Yeah," I said, sliding down off the bathroom counter. My leg brushed up against some part of Ryan, who was so still he could have been a statue.

"Why were you moaning?" he hiccuped. "And why are you in the … the…" he couldn't think of the name for it. The man was hammered.

"The dark," I offered.

"Yup. That's it," he slurred.

Goodness, his breath reeked.

Elijah was putting so much pressure on the knob, it shifted the door open wider. I put my foot behind it to hold it from opening any further.

Then, when Elijah reached for the light, I caught his hand.

"I have a terrible headache," I said, surprising myself with how fast I came up with the lie. "It must have been from the drinking, but having the light on makes it worse."

"Ohhhhh," he said, dragging the word out. "I was looking for Ryan, but I can't find him. He's missing his team get their asses handed to them."

"Maybe check outside. He may have gone to his car for something," I offered, touching my hand to my head again.

Elijah nodded, his unsteadiness almost causing him to bang his head against the door frame. He stumbled away, and I closed the door, afraid if I breathed too loud, he would come back and ask more questions.

Neither Ryan nor I moved an inch until we heard Elijah open the front door.

"Ryan, are you out here? Man, you're missing some major..." his words became indiscernible as he pulled the door closed behind him.

"You want me to finish?" Ryan whispered in the dark.

I did, but I wasn't going to. Elijah was outside, likely standing on or near the front lawn, and I suddenly remembered I hadn't watered the lawn today.

Now would be the perfect time to activate the sprinkler.

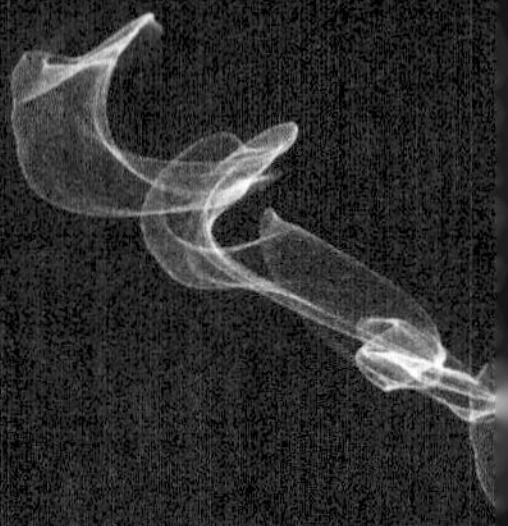

Day 4

TUESDAY
7:45 AM

"For the third time, Elijah. I didn't think I turned the sprinklers on. I thought I pressed the button that set the timer for tomorrow. You know the landscaper said it's best to water the lawn at least once or twice a week year-round."

Releasing the excess air from the plastic, I zipped the Peanut Butter and Jelly sandwich up into the ninja themed Ziploc bag for Grayson's lunch and placed it, along with his T-Rex mug, inside the Spiderman lunchbox.

The boy's themes were all over the place, but as long as the character was strong and mighty, Grayson wanted them.

Elijah's mouth twisted in annoyance as he stared at me and loosened his tie for the fifth time. He was obviously having trouble containing his displeasure with me.

I ignored him, thinking that if he undid that tie anymore, he would have to retie it completely.

He exited the kitchen without another word and I assumed, or rather hoped, he was leaving for work.

My phone vibrated, and I checked behind me to make sure Elijah hadn't mysteriously reappeared.

The message was from Nicole, and when I opened it, I felt as annoyed as Elijah had a few minutes ago.

It was the photos from a few days back when Elijah was spotted with... her.

Immediately filing the pictures away in a folder dedicated to proof of his perfidiousness, my mind went back to the first time I learned of this betrayal.

I'd heard Elijah reference her name once or twice when listening to the recordings, but I thought nothing of it.

However, it all hit me like a freight train one Wednesday afternoon when Nicole had notified me, questioning if Elijah and I had separated.

After I informed her we hadn't, her response was to send me several pictures of Elijah hugged up with his new woman.

I stared at the three photos for so long, my vision blurred. Or maybe it was the tears that did it.

A kiss shared between the two, him feeding her food from his plate and the one where he was affectionately holding her hand.

In each photo, her smile grew larger. The yellow dress she wore appearing to heighten her already joyful mood.

Having a visual of his affair was a hard pill to swallow, but I did, and now when I received pictures from Nicole, I filed them away, barely looking at them.

> Nicole: Sorry I forgot to forward you the pictures. Teenage girl drama is going to be the death of me.

> Bree: You're preaching to the choir. No worries though, thanks so much.

The one thing I couldn't understand was, as much as Elijah frequented this restaurant, how had he not noticed Nicole? She was only the mother of one of his daughter's closest friends, for goodness' sake!

And he had a nerve to tell Matteo that he was a dedicated father.

Jackass.

As soon as I put the phone down, Elijah returned to the kitchen, still ready to rumble.

"You are such an air head sometimes," he snapped. "Always forgetting things and messing up. You ruined my entire night!"

Facing him, I waited for him to get it all out. Clearly, he couldn't leave until he was done belittling me.

"I will be so glad when..." he abruptly broke off.

I glanced at the kids at the table, eating their breakfast. Lost in their own world. Zoey wearing headphones, Grayson flipping through a kid's magazine, and Ariel crushing her cheerios.

"When what?" I asked in a whisper.

Expectantly, Elijah didn't answer my question. He'd almost let it slip that he was divorcing me. Now he would get angrier just to cover his tracks. In three... two...

"Why in the hell are you whispering?" Elijah asked, right on schedule.

"I don't want the children to hear us," I said, motioning with my eyes.

Elijah briefly observed them. "They aren't paying us any attention," he said, pointing a finger in the general vicinity of the kitchen table. "And now, I" he shifted the finger to point at himself "am not paying you any attention."

He stormed off, calling me a fucking moron under his breath. I suppressed a smile. He was angry. And an angry man made mistakes.

1:30 PM

I entered Elijah's condo dressed like one of those spies from the old movies I love: Hat, sunglasses and a collared jacket.

I even wore gloves because it would be just my luck that I leave fingerprints and he hires some forensic team that finds it, proving I was there.

Admittedly, my thoughts were farfetched today, but I was taking no chances.

Ducking low and peeking around the corners of the one-bedroom condo revealed nothing and no one.

I already knew that Elijah wouldn't be here. He was at work and wouldn't return to this place until Sunday for his football party, if I remembered correctly.

Thomas, the building's janitor and the husband of one of the moms who helped me keep watch on Mr. unfaithful, had let me in. I knew Thomas wouldn't tell Elijah that I had been here, but I had to take all the precautions.

It still baffled me that Elijah thought I knew nothing about this place. I may have learned about it through the recordings, but there were other signs.

The way he was slowly moving stuff out of the house, claiming he needed it at work. The many nights he didn't come home because he "fell asleep at the office".

Or the sorry excuse he used when I found a receipt for his cable bill. He insisted he was paying a bill for a friend that had fallen on hard times, but I knew the truth.

I swear the man is too stupid to be cheating.

He needed to spend more time improving his lying skills. Then again, maybe he put no effort into the lies because he didn't care about the one he was lying to.

The thought made me furious.

Anyway, the highly expensive condo Elijah was renting was located thirty-five minutes from our home. He had made a substantial amount of changes since the last time I was here. A new couch and a giant flat screen tv.

What was that, 85 inches?

I turned towards the kitchen and noticed that there were also new blinds on the windows.

He could have simply kept the ones that came standard with the condo, but I'm sure he changed them because she, who shall not be named, preferred them.

Putting my rage aside for the moment, I began my inspection of the condo.

First scanning the kitchen cabinets, drawers and even the vents.

Next, I searched the living room. The small black coffee table had storage areas, but none of them held what I needed. I moved on to the TV stand and found nothing.

From there, I checked the bathroom, two small closets and underneath the bed.

Zilch.

Standing in front of the nightstand, I opened the drawer, pulled out a short stack of papers, and flipped through.

They were mostly contract drafts and receipts. Nothing stood out except one, a receipt for Shane's Vault Service and repair company from eight months ago.

The only vault that Elijah had was in his office at work and, if that is where he had stored the software, I was fucked.

Keep calm and stay focused.

There was no need to stress. If it wasn't here, the software was at home, not at his office. I could feel it.

Placing the papers on top of the nightstand, I resumed rummaging around the drawer. The contents were pretty bare.

Condoms, pencil, pack of gum, more condoms and...

What's this?

I held the small square image up. It was a picture of Elijah and her.

Automatically, my fist tightened, creating a deep crease within the photo. Realizing the picture could do more good if it was in one piece, instead of a million like I had intended, I pocketed it.

Walking back into the living room, I loved the space. It was really nice in here.

Big, roomy couch, fluffy carpeting and numerous shelves decorated with football memorabilia. This was a magnificent room for entertaining.

No wonder Elijah was having a football party here this Sunday, and from what I'd heard on the recording, it was going to be epic.

My eyes locked in on a shiny, gold football that sat on a shelf above the TV. It used to sit in his office at home, but like my husband, had found a new place to live.

I walked over and stretched my body up as far as possible, using the TV stand to give me a boost, and grabbed it from the shelf.

Adjusting the weight of it in my hand, I admired how heavy and sparkly the thick glass sculpture was.

Elijah's favorite football player's signature was scribbled at the top in black marker, easily making it worth hundreds, if not thousands, of dollars.

This thing had always been a dust magnet at home, and if I weren't wearing gloves, I'm sure it would be exceptional at collecting finger prints too.

I took a few giant steps back and assumed the football stance for a forward pass, then threw the ball as hard as I could at that impressive eighty-five inch screen.

It shattered instantly, and so did Elijah's cherished football souvenir, as it bounced off the coffee table, causing it to split into a million pieces.

Let's see you have a football party without a TV.

I wish I could see Elijah's face when he saw his beloved

items destroyed. What would he think happened? That the football fell off the shelf breaking the TV in the process? Or that someone broke in to ruin his life?

Ultimately, it made no difference.

It was time for me to leave before someone reported a loud crash and I got caught like a deer in headlights. Humming to myself, in a cheery mood, I headed to the front door, pulling my cellphone out of my pocket with plans to call Ryan.

However, when the phone rung in my hand, my nerves shot up, and I stopped walking. I knew this number.

"Hello?"

"Hi. Is this Mrs. Simmons?"

"Yes, this is she."

"This is Mrs. Slater, the principal at Zoey's school. We have a problem."

3:30 PM

"Zoey, I don't understand. Please tell me what happened again."

I gripped the steering wheel so tight my knuckles hurt.

My thirteen-year-old daughter had received a two-day suspension for calling a girl named Dylan Bowens a bitch and slapping her.

Currently, I didn't know why Zoey had done it. The facts were just as dicey and confusing as Zoey was behaving.

However, since Zoey refused to speak during the entire meeting, the principal used the rumors she'd heard to explain the story. There was a lot of he said, she said, but it all boiled down to a boy and sex.

Sex! My baby was having sex!

No, it was too early, way too early. Is that why she had been so moody? So distant?

I had tried talking to her, spending quality time, but Zoey was pulling away. And if I couldn't keep my own life in order, how was I supposed to save my darling daughter?

"I already told you, mom," Zoey said with so much attitude I wanted to shake her. "I don't like Dylan, so I hit her."

"Zoey, that is not how we behave. You don't just hit people! And sex! You are having sex?!"

My voice got much louder than I intended, but Zoey wasn't phased. She folded her arms and turned to stare out the window.

"Zoey," I said in the calmest voice I could manage. "Please do not ignore me when I am speaking to you."

"Just punish me alright," Zoey said.

Something was wrong. It had to be. I know teenagers were unpredictable, walking migraines these days, but this was still odd behavior.

"I don't want to punish you, Zoey. I want to know what is going on. So tell me now."

Silence.

"Now, Zoey!" I repeated sternly.

"It was about you, okay?" She shouted. "I hit Dylan because of you."

I was confused.

"What are you talking about, Zoey?"

"Dylan was teasing me because I said I wouldn't have sex with Mark."

I knew Mark. He was a nice young man that lived in the neighborhood. He and Zoey had been friends since they were five. In recent years, I'd suspected Zoey had developed a crush on him, but of course, she wouldn't confide in me.

Nevertheless, if someone had brought him up to tease her at school, my suspicions that she liked him were correct.

But she wouldn't sleep with him.

I was so relieved I tapped the brake, intending to slow down, but almost came to a full stop.

The car jerked and several cars behind me honked. I put up a hand to apologize and went back to trying to split my attention between my daughter and driving.

"Did you say you *wouldn't* sleep with him?"

I tried not to make my relief too noticeable, afraid she wouldn't keep talking, but she did.

"Yes. I didn't sleep with him and Dylan said that I was uptight and going to end up like my mom. A pathetic loser, with a husband that cheats on me because I'm some uptight good girl."

That little bitch.

I mean, the husband cheating part was true, but I was not some uptight good girl. I used to be, but still!

Kids were so cruel. So cruel and, sadly, maybe spot on. I stole a glance at Zoey before turning right onto our street.

She may be a teenager, but she was still my baby. Would always be my baby and she was suffering. Trying to fight back in a battle that she deserved no parts in.

I cursed Elijah again for doing this to our family. The problems between Elijah and I, should not affect our kids, yet they had, and they were.

I faced Zoey. "You know I don't condone violence." *Lord, please don't strike me down.* "But, I understand being so upset that you react before you think."

She looked at me, surprised by my levelheadedness.

"You can't make it a habit, though," I continued. "Even if it's defending me."

Zoey nodded, and her shoulders slumped.

"I'm sorry, mom. It won't happen again."

"It better not." I turned into our driveway and cut the car off. "Now, what do you think I should do with you concerning your two-day suspension?"

"I don't know," Zoey said. "I assumed you would lock me in my room and only feed me water and chicken nuggets."

Zoey hated chicken nuggets, always had. She was a weird kid, but sweet and usually soft-spoken. Sticking to herself and not bothering anyone.

That's when I had a brilliant idea.

"You know what?" I said. "I don't think you need to be inside. It's time you and I got outside."

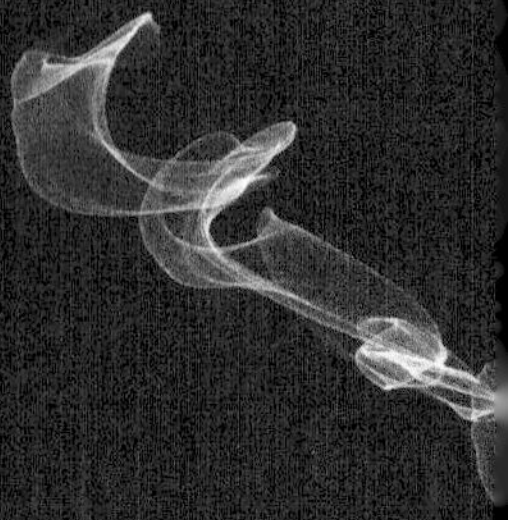

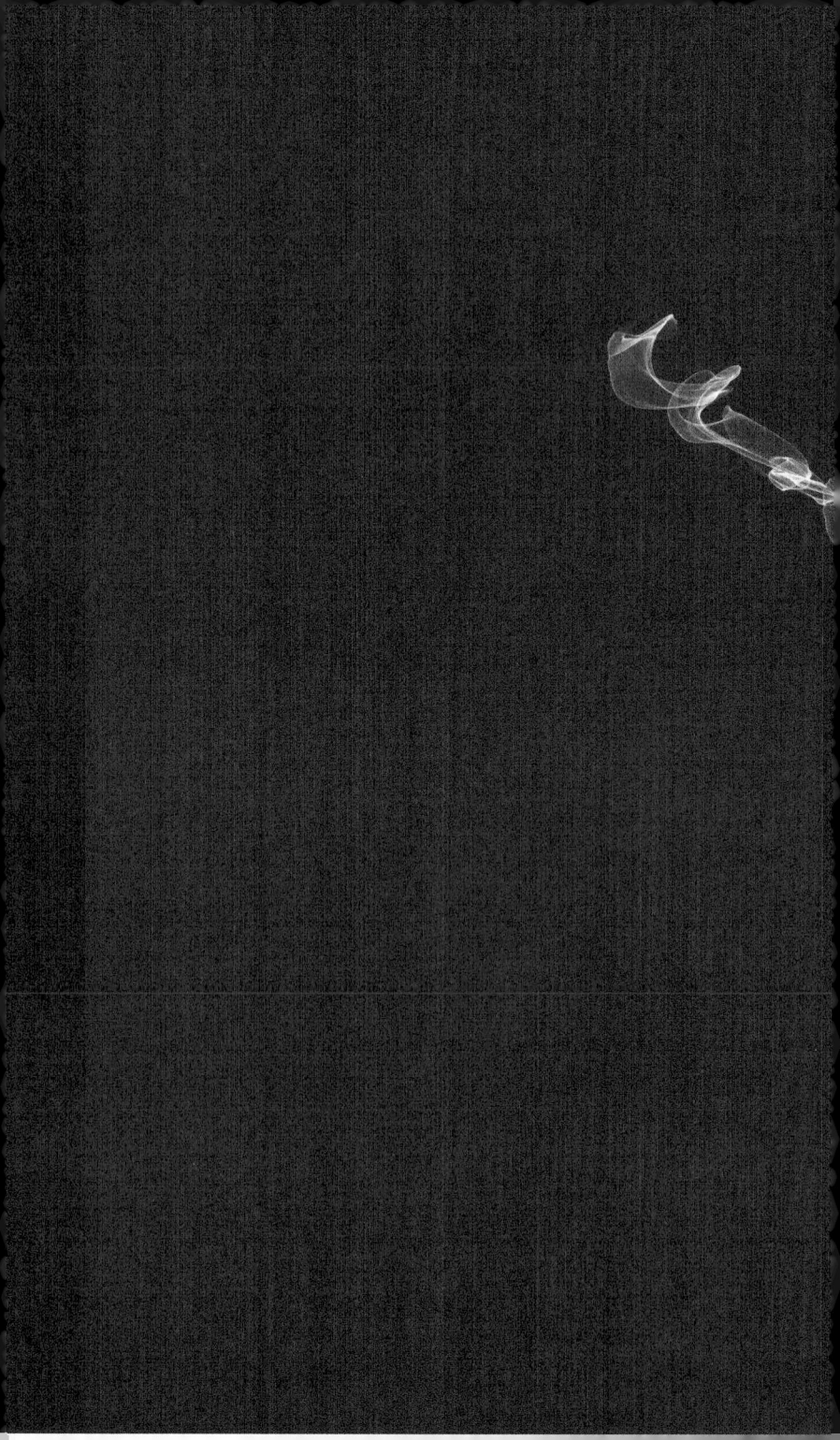

Day 5

WEDNESDAY
10:28 AM

"Come on mom, you said we could do it one more time!" Zoey shouted, smiling from ear-to-ear and pulling me forward.

This was exactly what I deserved.

I'd thought a fun day out at the theme park with Zoey bonding, sharing laughs and stuffing ourselves with funnel cakes was exactly what we needed.

Surely, this was a great way to make precious memories that would last a lifetime. However, I didn't realize that by doing so, it would be the end of *my* lifetime.

I felt like death's play toy. My legs burned, my body ached, I'd thrown up a little in the corner by the Icee stand and my head was still spinning from Rapto-Whirler.

That lying ass dinosaur.

He promised I'd have a roar of a good time. With how scrambled my brain felt, I'd be lucky if I still knew how to tell time!

But look at that face.

Zoey needed this. She needed me... and her father, but for now, I was all she had and I wouldn't let her down.

It took her some time to warm up when we first got here.

A day at the theme park with her mom wasn't exactly

what she would call a fun time. Actually, the look on her face upon entry swore that this idea was worse than any punishment I could have given her.

Nevertheless, after getting on a ride or two, she loosened up and unfortunately, so had my hip bone.

Was it creaking?!

I felt so old as Zoey dragged me back toward a whirly, twirly rollercoaster with colors and decor that reminded me of a monopoly board.

We'd already rode it one time, and I was not impressed. It lasted too long and moved too fast.

If I tried it again, I feared my body would skip go, and advance me straight to the geriatric stage.

We came to a sudden halt when Zoey spotted the sign in front of the giant rollercoaster. Her face transformed from cheery to sad.

"Aww man, it says the wait is forty-five minutes?"

Thank God. I needed a break.

"That's okay. I don't mind waiting."

As if she hadn't even heard me, those dark brown eyes that had just looked like she'd lost her best friend sparked back to life.

"I know, we can go to the flying ship! Come on, it's this way."

"Zoey," I said, pulling my arm back from her. "Let's take a break. I am starving, and I'm sure the world shouldn't be spinning right now."

Zoey gave me a self-conscious smile. "Sorry. There's a food stand over there. We can get burgers and fries."

"Now you're talking."

I threw my arm around her, mostly for balance, but also for love. She was growing up too fast and moments like these were scarce, so I would enjoy every second.

We ordered two burgers with everything on it and shared an enormous basket of fries while we talked about our favorite rides, movies, and memories.

I even got her to open up about more of the drama at school and her ever-growing crush on Mark.

Nailed it!

If anything made this day worth it, it was that, and now I could go to bed happy.

10:07 PM

I did not go to bed happy.

As a matter of fact, I probably wasn't going to bed at all. I was unsettled and likely to go into a smoking coma if things didn't change soon.

I had to find this software. If I didn't find it tonight, I was liable to walk straight up to Elijah and ask him where the hell it was.

I sat at the kitchen table, near the open window, cigarette smoke clouding all around me as I seethed with anger, listening to Elijah laugh through my earbuds.

Gianna had the nerve to be worried about what this situation was doing to her blood pressure.

Ha!

I was the one listening to these damn recordings and by the time it was all said and done, I, too, would be a candidate for medication.

I'd had to hit pause so many times, I lost count.

Currently, it was paused again because once Elijah said, *"I can't wait for this divorce to be over so that I can finalize the deal with my software."*

I saw red. It was not his software. It was my software.

My fucking software!

The cigarette shook in my trembling hand as I raised it to my lips, taking several long puffs while I imagined running Elijah over with my car.

The fantasy didn't give me enough real-life satisfaction, but finding the software would, so I put my cigarette down and pressed play again.

"If I'm unable to get it myself, you can come by and pick up the software for me. You know where it is."

Now we were getting somewhere. The software was still here, but with the divorce happening soon, that could change any day.

"Alright, Bree." I said aloud, giving myself a much needed pep talk. "Concentrate and listen very closely to everything he says."

"I don't know. Make up some excuse about needing to come by and then tell Bree you have to go to the bathroom or something. She isn't that bright."

My finger huddled over the stop button again after that insult, but I resisted the urge to press it.

That was until he said, *"Well, you know what I say. If the devil came knocking, you wouldn't let him in, unless he looked like a friend."* Then he laughed.

I stopped the tape and stared at the wall. My husband was pure evil.

As a young boy, his grandmother would often repeat that phrase to him, like a mantra.

It was a warning that sometimes the devil is the one you know. Often appearing in your life as someone you trust in order to get you to let your guard down.

I don't know who hurt her, but the woman was spot on.

Ironically, though, all she was doing was giving her grandson his life's motto, because Elijah had turned out to be the very monster she warned him to look out for.

Restarting the tape, I listened as Elijah droned on and on for a little while about nonsense, took several calls concerning work, and made more plans for the game on Sunday at his condo.

The look on his face when he saw his TV shattered would be priceless.

"Grayson! I told you to never come in without knocking. Get out of here!"

The sudden switch in tone, from casual to aggressive, when Elijah yelled at Grayson, pulled me back into focus.

I could hear Grayson's cries become more and more distant as he left the room and Elijah eventually closed the door.

"Sorry about that," Elijah said to whoever was on the phone. *"My damn son is always getting into something."*

I reminded myself to give Grayson an extra hug tomorrow.

As I continued to listen, I got up to grab a glass of wine. The cigarette was no longer cutting it as a solo act. It was time for backup.

Right after filling my glass to the rim with pinot noir. I heard something on the recording.

It was a low beep.

I'd heard it before in past recordings, but could never pinpoint exactly what it was because Elijah was always running his mouth or laughing at how brilliant he thought he was.

Stopping the tape, I rewound it back a few seconds.

Beep! Beep! Then Elijah laughing.

I released an annoyed groan and a huge cloud of smoke flowed from my lips and I put out my cigarette.

I know that sound, but from where?

When I replayed it this time, I increased the volume and held my breath, not even allowing my own breathing to interfere.

Beep! Beep! Beep! In quick succession, and then a low whistle.

My eyes lifted to the ceiling, then shifted toward the clock on the kitchen wall. Elijah wouldn't be home for another hour. I had to find out what that sound was.

It was pulling at me.

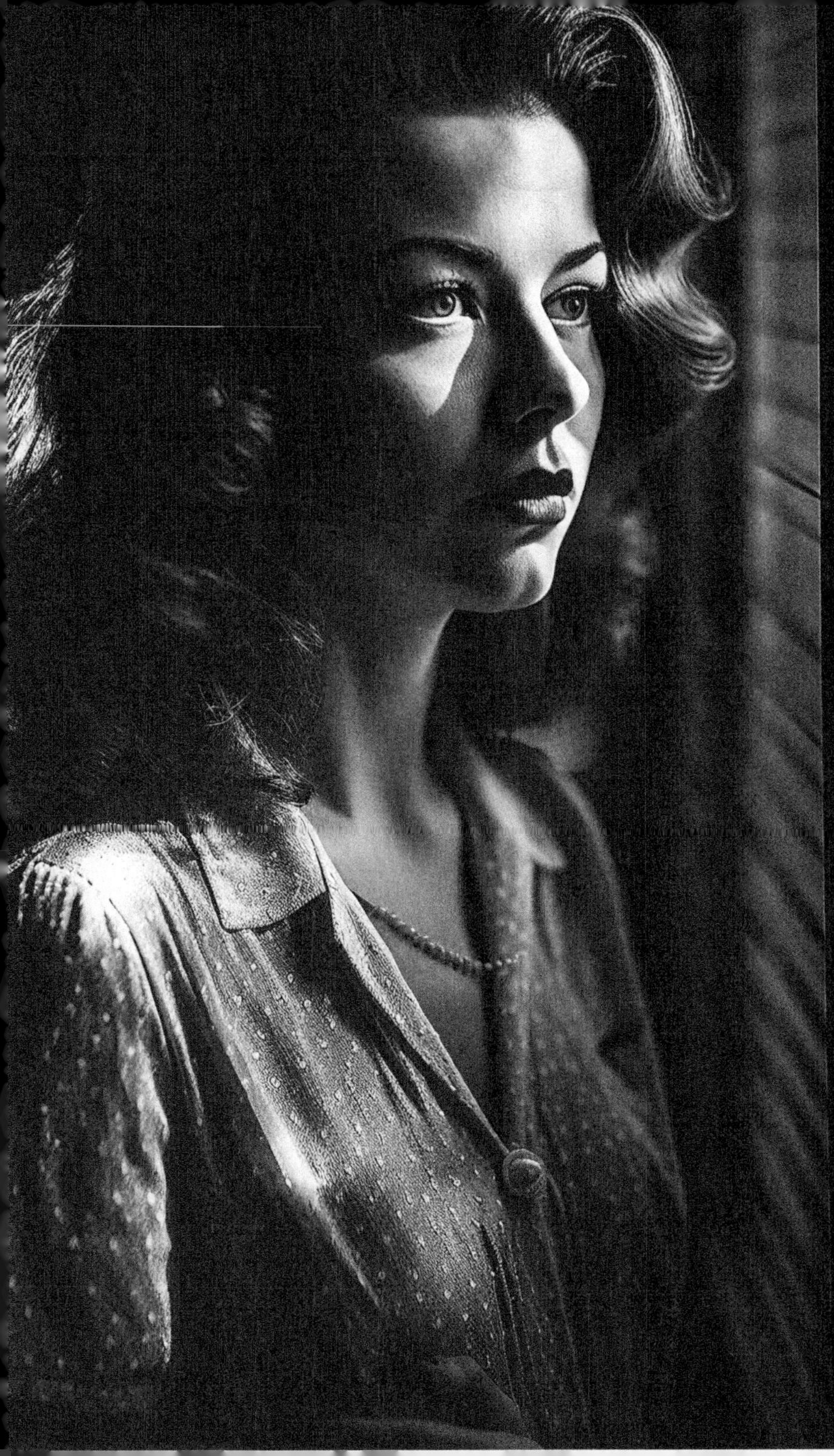

Discarding the evidence of my late night activities, I quietly made my way upstairs.

After checking on each kid to make sure they were sound asleep, I picked the lock and entered Elijah's office, closing the door behind me.

Now what?

For the first few minutes, I only stood there.

I had no idea what I was looking for. The sound I heard could be attributed to something on his computer, despite my intuition suggesting otherwise.

The office wasn't that big and held only a few things: a desk, a plant and two small tables.

Moving around slowly, I inspected the carpeted floor. There were no tears or disturbances to any of the edges.

As I slowly turned, my eyes thoroughly scanned the room, fixating primarily on the walls.

A picture of the five of us when we went to a company football game, five framed certificates announcing Elijah as agent of the year, a green and gold abstract painting, a framed autographed jersey from...

My eyes shifted back to the abstract painting.

It hung behind his desk and from here I noticed it was crooked and something dark peeked out

from the corner.

Walking over to it, I lifted the painting and carefully leaned it against the wall. I straightened to see what was behind it and my eyes almost bulged out of my head.

A safe!

"What the hell?" I nearly shouted, but reacted quickly by placing my hand firmly over my mouth to muffle any sound.

It remained there for another few seconds while I said a few more choice words that needed to be censored.

When did we get a safe?

There wasn't one when we moved into this house. I'd

know because I decorated every inch of it. Furthermore, when would Elijah have had the opportunity to install one?

The process must be noisy and time consuming. I couldn't understand when he would have had that type of freedom alone in this house.

If I'm not here, the kids are, and vice versa. The last time we all left the house was when we went on a trip to California eight months ago.

Suddenly, a recollection emerged in my mind.

That receipt I'd found at Elijah's condo from Shane's Vault Services and Repair. The date on it was from eight months ago.

"That son of a bitch!" I said under my breath.

With frustration building, I clenched my teeth and stared at the square black panel. I wasn't sure how big the safe was on the inside, but the front of it was no larger than 12x12.

It had a digital display screen with six dashes and a red light that kept flashing.

The impact of the situation left me feeling as though I'd been slapped. This husband of mine was a real piece of work.

His level of deception clearly had no limits, no conscience and no remorse. I was married to a monster.

A stinging sensation alerted me to the fact that I had been digging my nails into my palm. I stared at the imprints I'd made, while my mind and heart battled on which emotion I had time for.

Vengeance won out.

I could lick my wounds later. Right now, I needed a code, a six-digit code it seemed, and I was drawing a blank.

I thought of all the kids' birthdays in the pattern of two-digit months, two-digit days and two-digit years.

That could work, if it were my code, but it was Elijah, and it was unlikely that he would use their birthdays.

Hmm, maybe he'd use his own?

I stepped to the key panel, as the red light blinked incessantly, taunting me, I worked diligently to steady my trembling finger, fully aware that this could be an ominous sign, foreshadowing that my guess would ultimately prove to be incorrect.

Unperturbed, I entered the six numbers.

BZZZZZZZZZZZ!

My heart nearly thumped out of my chest and I took several steps back, feeling like I'd just selected the wrong answer on a game show.

The buzzing sound only lasted a second, but it was loud and threatening, warning me to watch it or else it would wake up the entire neighborhood.

Shit.

I had to get in this safe. I ran a hand through my hair, trying to think of Elijah's life in codes. Six digits that marked something that mattered to him.

Which was difficult because it was apparent that I knew so little. He lived with us, but apart from us at the same time.

Regularly making up excuses to stay away or leave early. I scanned the office again, walking back to the images on the walls for closer examination.

Maybe one of the dates on his agent of the year certificates would work, but I didn't think so. There were so many and I couldn't see him ranking one above the other.

I stopped in front of the picture of us together at the football game. If that was the date, then I was screwed. I didn't remember when we went there. All I remembered was that I was happy, even if the emotion was fleeting.

Personally, during that period, I was experiencing a great deal of turmoil. I faced the daunting task of making a life-changing decision after a particularly hard truth had been revealed.

Therefore, I welcomed a beautiful day with my family where everything was perfect.

Zoey was smiling so big, holding up a candy bar and a giant milk shake. She was ecstatic during the entire event, shoving in all the sugary foods she could handle.

However, when we got home, she had a major stomach ache and didn't even want to look at anything sweet for an entire month.

Ariel was in my arms, only five months at the time, hugging my face with her slobbery hands.

She wasn't able to walk, but insisted on trying it all day by attempting to wriggle free from my arms every time we climbed or descended the stadium stairs.

I guess go big or go home was her motto.

And there was Grayson. Handsome and high energy. He was striking a pose like a ninja. My magnificent son had always been obsessed with being a superhero or spy.

"Mom, what's eight plus two?" Grayson's voice sounded off in my head.

Those mathematical spy questions he asked me repeatedly. I assumed they were from his cartoon, but what if they weren't?

My eyes darted to the safe.

What if he'd seen something, or rather, spied something?

"Ten," I said quietly, answering myself.

I walked over to the safe and entered the two digits.

"And what is ten plus seven?"

I entered seventeen.

"And finally seventeen plus twenty-two?"

I pressed the three and then held my breath before hitting the nine.

Beep! Beep! Beep!

I put my hand to my chest and gawked at the green light. Looks like I'd found the source of the beeping noise.

"We're the best super spies ever!" I said, a single tear rolling down my cheek. "Thank you, Grayson."

I pulled the lever and almost sank to my knees when I saw what was inside.

My software!

The intensity of the joy I felt was so overwhelming it briefly left me unable to move, forcing me to simply gaze at it in awe.

The search for what had always been mine was over.

Breaking free of my haze, I stepped forward and meticulously went through the contents of the safe, collecting everything I needed.

Next, I inserted my software into the computer and made a few minor changes.

And because I was now in such a marvelous mood, I planted a little more evidence on Elijah's computer for a side project I was working on.

I sat back in the chair and smiled. Revenge felt so good.

Gathering my things, I logged off the computer and headed to the door.

After giving the room one last visual inspection to make sure everything was in place, I turned off the light and exited quietly.

Brace yourself, Elijah, the real fun is about to begin.

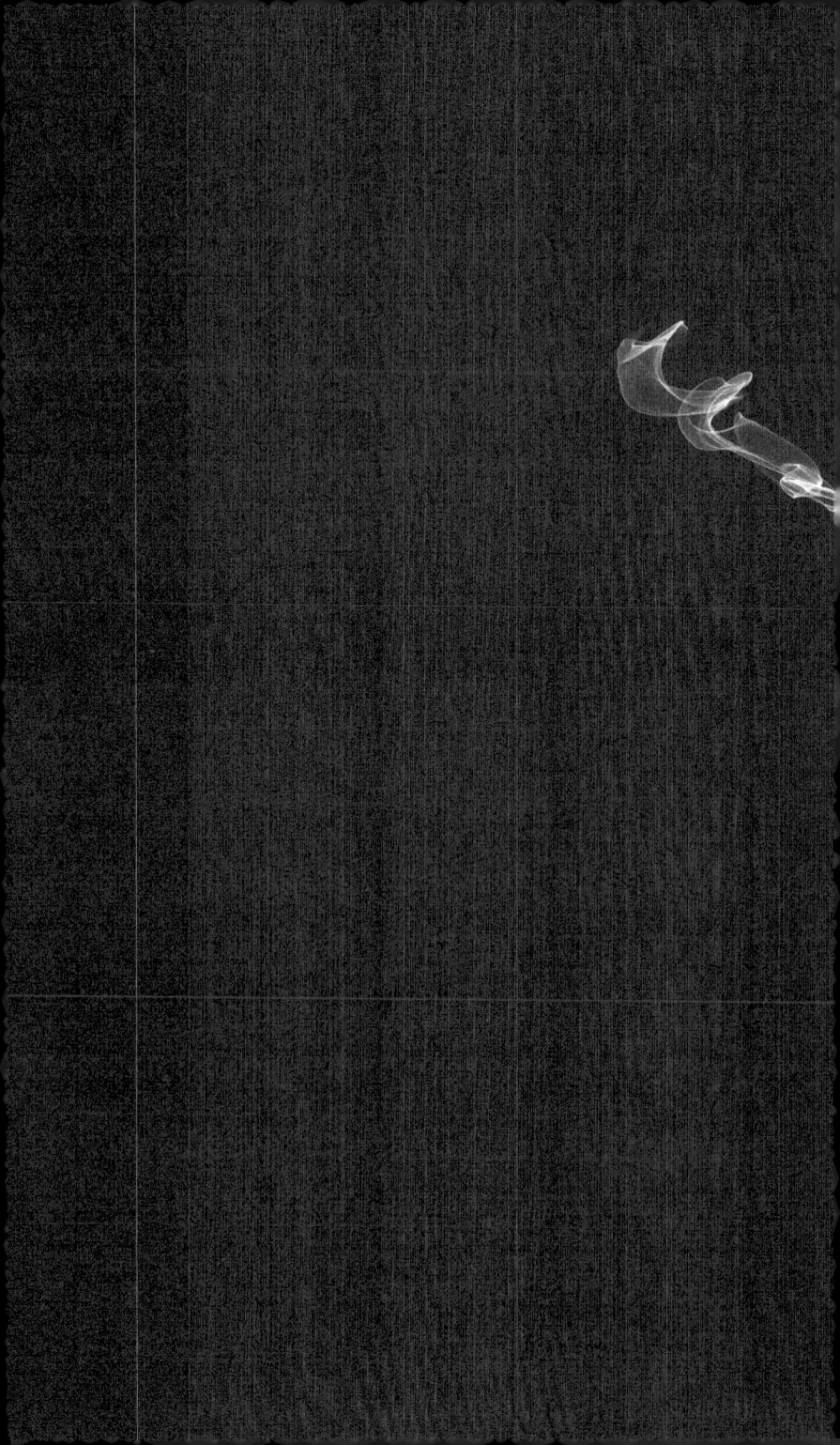

Day 6

THURSDAY
7:15 AM

I placed two heart-shaped pancakes onto Grayson's plate, then kissed him on the cheek.

His dark brown eyes grew wide with excitement.

"These are my favorite pancakes, mom!" Then he seemed to consider the treat, trying to determine the reason behind my kindness. Suspiciously, he asked, "What's the occasion?"

"Just because," I said, smiling without restraint.

"I don't think my report card is going to make you as happy as you think."

I laughed.

"Don't worry, Grayson, I'm not holding anything against you." *You simply helped mommy find her software and now your father is going to experience his own personal hell.* "I just wanted to do something special for you," I added.

"Works for me," he said with a shrug and dug in.

Ariel lifted half of her pancake in the air and offered it to me.

"I love you, mommy," she said. "This is half of my heart. You can have it."

I touched my hand to my chest.

"I love you too, sweetie. But you can keep it. I want you to enjoy your breakfast."

"Can't. Got to go poop," she said, sliding down from her chair.

That sweet moment was ruined.

Ariel hurried away, dancing and singing a song about poop that she'd learned from a potty training video.

"Good job. I'm so proud of you," I called out as Ariel slammed the bathroom door shut.

Got to cheer them on at every turn.

I loved my kids so much. They can be quirky, moody, loud, and even obnoxious, but they're mine.

Having love on the brain shifted my thoughts to the man I loved. My fingers automatically traced the white gold Heart Pendant around my neck.

YOU ARE MY EVERYTHING,
- LOVE, R

Is what the small card inside had read, and the feeling was mutual.

Today was our four-year anniversary. Four long years of sneaking around behind Elijah's back, stealing quick moments in the office, at his place, my place, or wherever else we could manage.

In the midst of how crazy things had become, I thought he'd forgotten that today was our anniversary, but he hadn't.

The necklace arrived an hour ago via UPS, a perfect start to my day.

My heart not only filled with butterflies and giddiness, but a mountain of relief, because Elijah wasn't home to see me receive it. He would question who it was from and why they sent it.

I was in too good of a mood to come up with a lie.

Luckily for me, Elijah didn't even come home last night.

He texted around midnight that he was "caught up with a client" and I left it at that. There was no need to respond.

Instead, I called Ryan and basked in the ambience of his heartwarming words, as he told me all the lovely things I needed to hear to maintain my focus on achieving my goal. Shortly after, we said goodnight, and I woke up to this.

The most beautiful piece of jewelry I had ever seen.

It was so lavish, alluring and majestic that I almost didn't want to wear it. The fear that I'd destroy the diamonds or have the necklace accidentally ripped off by Ariel was a genuine concern.

Which is why I simply tucked it back into my shirt, where it would be safe and close to my heart.

No, Elijah wasn't missed at all. Besides, later tonight I planned to see him and it wouldn't be pretty.

My phone vibrated in my pocket with a text from Pam. She wanted to confirm that I was coming over in an hour. I needed to use her computer again to email all the documents I'd collected to my attorney.

I confirmed I would be there and turned my attention to the outside.

Through the window I could see the grayish sky, filled with dark clouds. It was going to rain today. Possibly even storm and on many levels that was very fitting for what was to come.

My hand automatically went back to my necklace. It gave me comfort, strength and a tangible reminder that love always prevailed.

"Mom, I'm about to head to the library," Zoey said, before finishing her juice.

I turned toward her, blinking a few times to clear my thoughts. Zoey still had one more day of suspension to serve, but she also had a project due when she returned.

Showing major maturity, she'd asked if she could spend

the day at the library completing her portion so that her teammates Zara and Cassidy didn't have to complete her part and theirs as well.

"I'm proud of you and admire your commitment, Zoey."

One side of her mouth lifted in a half smile.

"I'm only doing what you would do, mom. Taking my responsibilities seriously."

I pulled her in for a hug. It was at these moments that I felt rewarded. To see all of my sacrifice, lecturing and patience pay off was what motherhood was all about.

Zoey stacked her books on the kitchen counter and pulled on her jacket.

"Are you sure you don't want me to drive you?"

"No, mom. The library is only five minutes away, and I have walked there many times, remember?"

I remembered, but I was feeling like a mother hen wanting to protect my little chick. It was all her fault for getting me into my feelings with how mature she was behaving.

"Alright, and Cassidy's mom is still bringing you home?"

"Yes," Zoey said, picking up her books.

"And you have money and your phone in case of an emergency?"

"Yes, mom," Zoey said, the teenage annoyance seeping back in.

I snapped my fingers. "Oh, and it might rain. Be sure to take an umbrella."

"Mom," Zoey said, halting me from saying anything else.

"Yes, honey," I answered with a gentle smile. Expecting anything except what came next. "Thank you," Zoey said.

That caught me off guard.

"For what?" I asked.

"Yesterday. I know I was supposed to be on punishment, but it was nice, just the two of us."

Darn it!

Once more, a flood of motherly emotions overwhelmed me. I wrapped my arms around her and squeezed until she protested.

Holding her at arm's length, I said, "I'll make sure we do it again soon."

"I'd like that," she replied and left, but I remained standing there.

My babies deserved the world, along with a mother and a father that loved them and soon they would have it.

No lies, no deceit, and no Elijah.

6:23 PM

I'd just exited Elijah's office, completing a very crucial step in my plan called the old switcheroo.

The bag that I carried contained everything necessary for things to progress smoothly, and I would drop it off before heading to the restaurant.

This was going to be so good.

Placing the bag on my bedroom dresser, I entered my walk-in closet in search of the perfect thing to wear. Mentally, I had already settled on two outfits, but I needed to see them side-by-side to make a final decision.

As I stood before the full-length mirror, I meticulously compared both outfits, attempting to discern which one would elicit the correct emotions from the crowd.

The first was a dress that made me look like one of the old-fashioned housewives I used to see on the TV commercials.

It was a red and black swing dress with retro button stitching and black and white polka dot print.

It was certainly elegant and did the trick if I were in a vintage mood, but I think for this occasion it made me appear overly polished.

The second option was significantly simpler; Stained washed jeans and a light gray sweater.

It was my unofficial mom uniform for when I took Grayson to soccer games. The jeans were torn and thinning in random areas, while the sweater displayed a stain on the left shoulder that refused to wash out no matter what I used.

If I were to choose this one, it would give people the impression that I am overwhelmed with tasks and not appreciated for my efforts.

In other words, this outfit was the winner.

I got dressed, studied myself in the mirror, and frowned. The clothes were perfect but the hair could use some work.

Currently, my hair was pulled back into a neat ponytail. It needed to be much wilder.

Therefore, leaving the ponytail intact, I pulled a few random strands of hair loose, and finally the look came together.

I was going to Atlas, a five-star restaurant with impeccable service and a luxurious atmosphere, after all. It was important that I put the extra effort into my appearance.

My phone chimed with a message from Nicole.

> Nicole: He's here near the window. Come whenever you're ready.

I smiled at my reflection. Oh, I was ready. But not to dine, to destroy.

7:45 PM

I walked into the restaurant, squeezing past the crowd of people huddled near the front door, waiting to be seated.

A few exquisitely dressed patrons eyed me, whispering to

themselves or others in their party about what I was wearing or if I'd accidentally came to the wrong place, but I ignored them.

Instead of judging me, they should be thanking me. I was about to give them a show.

Known for its grandeur and exclusivity, Atlas stood as one of downtown's largest and most elite restaurants. Although I had never dined here before, I decided at this very moment to add it to my list.

After a hostess wearing a long black dress led a large group to the back, Nicole came into view.

She was speaking with two guests that must have been extremely angry. The man was swinging his arms around and pointing at himself, while the woman was pointing at Nicole and speaking at the same time.

They were shouting, but from where I stood, surrounded by other guests lost in their own conversations and the subtle sound of jazz, it was difficult to make out what they were saying.

Nicole's body language was relaxed and her hands were up, palms out, in a universal gesture used to de-escalate an aggressive situation.

Not wanting to miss my window of opportunity, I almost went over to see if I could help, but a manager showed up and Nicole slowly took a few steps back to let him handle the irate guests.

Once she noticed me, Nicole gives me a slight nod, and I make my way back to the dining area.

A few people stared as I walked by.

My denim jeans and stained sweater were not suitable for the dress code of this place, but I hold my head high and keep on walking.

I make a left turn, weaving my way through the tables, heading toward those lining the window.

Even though I was on a mission, I couldn't help but notice all the lovely couples holding hands, confessing their love, and sharing food.

It was all so nauseating, but I refrained from rolling my eyes by reminding myself that everyone wasn't here to confront their cheating husbands.

After passing several tables filled with more couples and various other group sizes, I spot Elijah and his date about five tables up ahead.

There is a party of eight seated at the table across from Elijah's, and one guest is a senior citizen.

Grandma, as I have already mentally named her, is wearing a colorful sweater with her hand adjusting the nozzle on the oxygen tank nestled against her chair.

Take a few deep breaths for me, too, grandma.

I'm now less than twenty feet away, my eyes locked on Elijah. He is facing me, but doesn't yet notice me.

His date, the treacherous bitch, is wearing a slutty, spaghetti-strapped dress and sporting a fancy updo that gathers into a neat bun at the top of her head.

Although her back is to me, I can hear her laughing hysterically at something Elijah said, and my blood boils.

Suddenly he looks up, and the moment his eyes meet the fury in mine, they nearly bulge out of his head, and he drops his fine linen napkin.

Slowly getting to his feet, Elijah extends his hands as if it will extinguish my wrath.

"Bree I can..." Before he finishes his sentence, I reach out and grab the fluffy bun at the top of his date's head and yank her to the floor.

She screamed and the entire restaurant went silent.

Utensils dropped, toasts ceased, and grandma placed the oxygen mask over her mouth and nose and took several deep breaths.

I looked down into the shocked and guilty eyes of my cousin Pam. Her once elegant bun was now nothing more than a mess of hair sticking out from the side of her head.

Showtime.

"Bree, let me explain," she said, her palms planted against the floor, holding her up.

"Shut the fuck up!" I yell. "What can you explain? Are you going to explain why you, my cousin, my closest family member, has been fucking my husband behind my back?"

Gasps sounded throughout the restaurant, creating an atmosphere of tension and fear. In a state of panic, Pam opens her mouth, but no sound comes out.

I could practically see the wheels turning in her mind, trying to find something to say that wouldn't land one of those crystal wine glasses upside her head.

I'd just seen her a few hours ago.

And if I weren't so committed to playing the long game when it came to setting Elijah's world on fire, I would have stabbed her then.

Pam shook her head, her face turning as red as the dress she was wearing.

"I... it was..."

I snatched up a steak knife from the table and pointed it at her.

"Stop talking," I gritted in a low snarl.

Whispered conversations spread throughout the room, and people pulled out their camera phones, ready and willing to document my pain.

Technology has made us such a lovely society, I thought sarcastically.

I spun around, knife still in hand, and faced Elijah. He was frozen over his chair as if he couldn't decide if he should sit down or stand up.

"And you," I spat. "You bastard. Too busy to help me take

care of your children, too busy to play soccer with your only son, too caught up in work to ever come home, but you make time to stick your dick in a woman that I know for a fact had chlamydia at least three times!"

I think it was at that moment that grandma died briefly. Out of my peripheral I saw her slump back in her chair, but woke again suddenly when a woman at the table shook her.

"Bree," he cautioned, his hand locking onto the edge of his table while his tie hung so low it was inches away from dipping into his soup. "I can explain."

"Don't even try it," I warned.

I heard a commotion and could see a man in a suit coming toward me up ahead. Dropping the knife back onto the table, a tear that wasn't part of the show slid down my cheek.

"All I ever tried to do was love you and this is how you repay me," I said in a defeated tone.

"Bree, I'm... I'm sorry," he stuttered.

I didn't respond. The restaurant's manager, Gregory, as the name tag revealed, had arrived.

Obviously, having heard enough to know what had occurred, his eyes filled with sympathy as he laid a gentle hand on my shoulder.

"Ma'am, you are going to have to leave," he said.

I didn't move, and the whole restaurant remained silent in anticipation of what I would do next.

"Please," Gregory whispered.

He hated to do it, but he had a business to run. Understandably, he couldn't in good conscience let me murder two low-lives right in front of him.

Reluctantly, I turned on my heel.

As I exited, dinner guests followed my every movement, still recording, just in case there was more drama to unfold.

It occurred to me that people were likely to share this event on their social medias and it would spread like wildfire.

Truthfully, I hoped it did because what good was revealing Elijah's deep dark secrets, if I couldn't share it with the world.

Day 7

FRIDAY
9:07 AM

The sound of dresser drawers being opened and closed woke me up. I popped one eye open and glanced at the clock. No one should be here.

I'd dropped the kids off at school and daycare two hours ago and had returned home to take a nap. I was nursing a slight hangover from drinking too much the night before.

I sat up in bed and there was Elijah, still wearing his suit from his date last night, minus the jacket and tie, placing clothes in a large duffle bag.

"What the hell are you doing here?" I asked, tossing the covers back and jumping out of bed.

The comforter stubbornly clung to my left foot and ended up slipping off the bed as I got up. It weakened the emphasis of my anger regarding his presence, but I was back in full effect within seconds, stomping over to him.

"Shouldn't you be at Pam's house?"

Elijah stopped placing clothes in the bag and stared at me like I was the one in the wrong.

"Real funny," he said without humor. "First you embarrass me in public and then you assume that there is still something going on between Pam and I."

"Less than 24 hours ago there was, and if you think I

would believe you now, when you lied to me in the first place, it's obvious you and her are sharing a brain."

"I didn't plan it, it just happened alright. You are always so ready to make me the bad guy."

My head jerked back in shock. "You are the bad guy!" I screamed.

"See! I can't be civilized with you. What happened with Pam wasn't planned. No one was trying to hurt you. We simply had too much to drink one night and things got out of hand. It wasn't even serious."

Angry tears stung my eyes.

"And that is supposed to make it better? What is it with you? Are you running out of women to have an affair with? She is my cousin, Elijah!" I exclaimed. "How could you?"

This time when he glanced at me, I swore the slightest bit of remorse shown in his eyes. I noticed it because Elijah was never remorseful.

Possibly for a split second all he had done and was planning to do to me actually penetrated that stone cold heart of his. Nevertheless, it was gone now, and he was back to defending himself.

"Nothing I did was intentional. She came on to me."

"Oh poor you," I mocked. "Does lying never exhaust you?"

"Typical, Bree. You never listen and you always play the victim."

I folded my arms across my chest. "Are you even sorry?"

He exhaled loudly, as if the question were ridiculous.

"Of course, I'm sorry, Bree."

"You don't act like it. You haven't even said it once."

"Because you don't want an apology, you just want to argue and fight."

He had a point. His apologies were futile at this stage in our marriage.

Elijah shook his head dismissively and went back to packing. He reached for a blue shirt that I had given him a few years ago as an anniversary gift. It was made from a high-quality fabric and had his initials threaded into the pocket.

Bastard!

I bumped the drawer hard with my hip, slamming his hand inside.

"Are you fucking crazy!" he yelled, clutching the injured hand.

"I don't know Elijah, am I? If so, you made me this way. Now, get out!"

"I don't have to deal with this shit," he said, bending down in preparation to close the duffle bag. "You are really losing it."

Man, are you in for a treat. I've already lost it.

Elijah made several attempts to zip up the bag, failing each time because his injured hand wasn't cooperating properly.

I stood there with my arms crossed, so aggrieved that I was shaking.

Keeping my rage contained took an effort I didn't think I was capable of. I felt like a bottle of soda that had been shaken up and Elijah was set on removing the top.

Not yet. It's not time yet.

Thinking of the last time I had to be extremely patient in order to exact my revenge on someone mollified me.

I was in high school, and the recipient of my pay back was Daisy Ramirez. It took all school year, but things didn't end well for her and they would not end well for Elijah.

Finally getting the bag closed, he yanked it up and stormed out of the bedroom. I followed him, wanting to slam and lock the front door behind him. However, he didn't make a left towards the stairs; he kept straight.

"You missed the turn for the stairs," I called out to him. "I said I want you out of here."

He ignored me, walking instead to his office, pulling a key out of his pocket and unlocking the door in one smooth motion. I guess his hand wasn't hurting that much.

Dammit, I should have used my foot.

Elijah slammed the door shut before I could speed up enough to stop him.

"Get out, Elijah, or else I am going to call the cops to have you removed."

I wasn't calling anyone, not now, anyway.

Things were about to get interesting. Elijah continued to ignore me and I kicked the door a few more times for theatrics. Then I put my ear against the smooth wood.

A scraping against the wall... *the painting is down.*

Three beeps... *the safe is open.*

And then... "What the fuck?"

The thunderous voice of a man who'd just been ripped clean off penetrated through the door and I grinned. This didn't make up for all he'd done, but it was a good start.

Clicking, clacking, and knocking sounds were heard before I forced myself away from the door.

Moments later Elijah yanked it open, eyeing me as I stood there with my arms crossed and tapping my foot, glaring coldly.

The door was opened wide enough for me to see that he'd put the painting back on the wall.

"Have you or the kids been in my office?"

How dare him!

"Seriously, that's what you want to know? If someone has been in your damn office?"

"Answer the question," Elijah spat.

The man was furious. There was a noticeable twitch in his right eye, and his hands were tightly balled into fists. I'd always known Elijah had a bad temper, however never in our marriage had he hit me.

Was today going to be the day?

If so, I wasn't afraid. Let that spineless bastard give me a reason to end his life.

I took a step closer, itching to poke the bear.

"Maybe you should ask Pam if she has been in your precious office," I said through gritted teeth. "Last time. Get out or I am calling the cops."

This time, I wasn't bluffing. I'd seen the reaction I needed to see and after all of this shouting, the headache from my hangover had rebuilt itself with a vengeance.

Elijah heard me. I know he did, but something was off. His eyes were on me, but they were vacant, like a dark cloud that signaled a storm was on its way. He wasn't seeing me at all and I knew then that trouble was coming.

His mind was somewhere else, on someone else, and I'd bet I could guess who.

Without another word, he spun around, locked the office door, and pushed past me. I watched him leave, narrowing my eyes slightly at something peeking out from the top of his bag.

Was that his gun case?

He headed downstairs and exited through the front door, slamming it so loud that the walls shook.

I had it wrong. Trouble wasn't coming; it had already arrived.

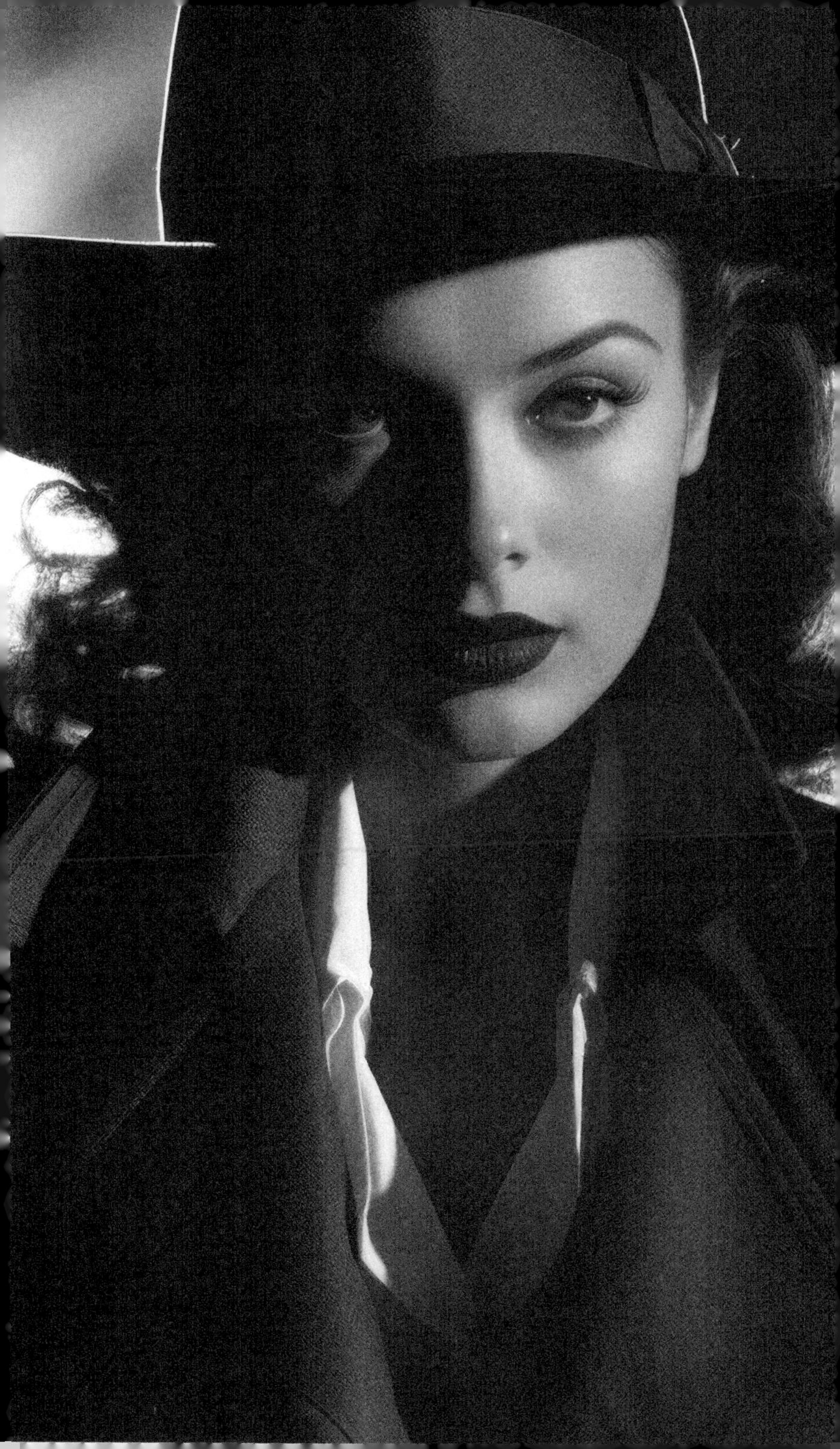

11:30AM

"I miss you," Ryan said.

"I miss you, too," I replied seductively, my thoughts recalling a very sexy scene.

I hadn't told Ryan about Pam and Elijah.

Talking about it made it worse. Which was why I had only told Gianna the basics of what happened and avoided the deep dive that would consist of facts and feelings.

"You could sneak up here and see me," Ryan said. "Elijah isn't in the office."

"Wait," I said, facing away from the kids. "He's not at work?"

"No, I haven't seen him today."

That was odd. When he left this morning. I knew he was angry, but I still thought he would go to work. He loved work more than me and his kids combined.

Pulling a paper towel off the roll, I dried my hands and watched Ariel and Gianna's twins spill pink paint all over my kitchen table.

Gianna was trying to keep them in line, but she was outnumbered and Ariel, the ringleader of "let's paint with our hands," was not for the weak.

My phone beeped for the tenth time, indicating a call on the other line. I didn't have to check to know that it was Pam calling.

It had been Pam calling all last night, throughout the entire morning, and apparently it would still be Pam calling for the rest of this evening.

Ignoring the unwelcome distraction, I opened the cabinet to collect plates and cups for the food that would arrive soon.

"Do you want me to come over and hang out with you?" Ryan asked.

"Not now," I said, declining the tempting offer to be comforted. "Gianna and her kids are over, so it wouldn't be a good idea."

"Alright Babe, only if you're sure because I could hide in the bushes until they leave."

I paused again from pulling plates down from the cabinet and smiled. He was fantastic at making me feel special and loved. Elijah should take lessons from him.

"No, I just ordered a pizza, but maybe..." I added in a whisper, checking over my shoulder to be sure that no one was within earshot before continuing. "You can come over later tonight, around eleven. Gianna should be gone, and the kids will be asleep."

"You know I'll be there."

"Great. I'll leave the back door open."

I expected Ryan to make a joke at my sexual innuendo, but Ariel came running over to me.

"Mommy! Mommy!"

Her hands were outstretched and covered in paint.

"Gotta go, the boss needs me. Love you."

"Love you too," he said.

I disconnected my bluetooth and lifted Ariel into the air, just in time to prevent my clothes from being dyed by her little hands.

"Yes, sweetie," I said, spinning her around a few times before carrying her over to the kitchen sink. I turned on the water and grabbed the dishwashing liquid.

"Aww mom, I'm not ready to stop painting," she whined.

"I know, but the pizza is almost here and you don't want pink pizza, do you?"

Her eyes widened with the possibility.

I sometimes forgot how enticing insane things sounded to a toddler.

The paint rinsed off her hands easily and flowed down the

drain, just like every time. It was the only reason I allowed her to paint.

It was her favorite hobby, but if it wasn't easy to remove, she could forget about it because I wasn't letting her paint my entire house pink.

"What did you want to tell me?" I said, hoping to interrupt the thought of animated pink pizza slices dancing around in her head.

Suddenly remembering, Ariel kicked her legs to get down. I dried her hands and put her down.

"I wanted to show you the picture I painted of you."

She took my hand and led me toward the kitchen table.

When we got there, Gianna was wrestling the purple paint out of Lucia's, *or was it Gia's,* hands? They were identical twins and even though I'd known them since birth, I still got them mixed up from time to time.

"Way to hold down the fort," I said to Gianna, my eyes quickly darting to the giant mess covering the kitchen table, then back at her.

Gianna swiped at her forehead, transferring the orange paint from her hand to her face.

"Listen, you try controlling three kids that you dosed up on sugar just to get them to leave you alone for five minutes and then realized after they are running circles around you, it was a bad idea."

"Good point," I said.

"Here's the picture mommy, don't you look beautiful?"

Ariel offered me a green piece of construction paper that had three of her pink handprints on it.

"I sure do," I said, turning the picture upside down, sideways, and face down before returning to the direction she initially gave it to me in. "But where's my face?"

She laughed as if I were a comedian.

"Mommy, your face is right there," she said, pointing at the handprint in the middle.

"And where are my eyes, nose, and mouth?"

"Right there," Ariel responded, pointing at the hand in the middle again. Then, moving on to point to the second and third handprints, she said, "That is one ear, and that is your other ear."

She'd now explained why there were three hand prints. They represented my face and ears, but I still wasn't getting it.

"Well, now it's just a face and two ears. I still don't see the eyes, nose or mouth."

Ariel had the nerve to let out a long sigh, like she was explaining a Picasso to an imbecile. I was almost offended enough to tell her that I wasn't the one high off of nontoxic paint. According to this painting, she was.

"See the lines on your face?"

I looked closer. I saw three small black dots almost in the shape of an upside-down triangle.

"Yeah, I see it."

"That's your eyes and nose. You don't need a mouth because pictures don't talk."

"Uh huh, I see now," I said, continuing the conversation, using her logic as the baseline. "But why are my ears the same size as my face, but everything else is so small?"

"Because you have a big head and big ears," she said gleefully.

Out of the mouth of babes.

They never tell you that once you escape bullies in high school, your own children will become your new tormentors. This conversation had the potential to land me in a therapist chair, triggered from a drawing made by my three-year-old.

I was going to stop while I was ahead.

"Thank you, Ariel," I said, holding the painting to my chest. "I will treasure this forever."

Ariel ran off, going to join the handcuffs in the backyard, and Gianna and I exchanged a shrug and a sigh of relief.

The kids were busy, which meant that we were in the clear and could finally talk.

Gianna opened her mouth to speak, and two things happened simultaneously.

Gia came back inside and my cellphone rang.

I quickly hit the button to silence my phone.

"Mom! You said you would come out and play with us. We need an evil queen to tie up," Gia said with so much sass she reminded me of a mini Gianna.

"Yes, but I am speaking to Mrs. Bree right now. Let your sister be the evil queen."

"Ugh!" Gia said, exasperated. "The queen needs to be old and you're old! So you fit better."

Our kids were sure doing a number on our self-esteem today.

I looked at Gianna empathetically.

"I have a big head and ears," I offered.

"I'd rather have that than to be old," Gianna groaned, getting to her feet. "I'll be back in ten minutes."

With annoyance, she walked toward the back door. Giving Gia her list of demands as they exited. "I will be your evil queen, but don't put any dirt on me like you did last time."

I laughed, shaking my head as my phone rung, yet again!

This time I snatched it up and in a bitter tone said, "You've got some nerve."

"Thank God you answered," Pam said with so much relief I almost felt bad... almost.

"Why do you keep calling? I have nothing to say to you."

"Bree, please. You can't shut me out like this. You are the only family I have."

"That's funny," I said, "because that didn't seem to matter to you when you were screwing my husband."

"Bree, it was a mistake. A stupid, stupid mistake."

I went on in my rant as if I hadn't even heard her.

"Why would you even want him after all he has put me through?"

"I was having a weak moment, okay? I'd just broken up with Dylan. I was crying and feeling hopeless. I ran into Elijah at the store and things just spiraled out of control from there. I wanted to break it off every time I saw him. I am so sorry."

"Gee, an apology. That makes it all better," I said sarcastically.

"Please believe me."

I let her words sink in.

Pleading words coming from the person I'd known all my life. I'd cried on her shoulders, celebrated my wins, and used her encouragement to get through my losses.

Pam was practically my sister, which meant that it was my sister, who'd slept with my soul-less husband.

An extreme pressure assaulted my chest, and I had to stop thinking and concentrate on breathing. The devastating sensations were triggered by pure rage, or a broken heart. Probably both.

Six months ago, when I learned about Elijah's schemes, I'd requested the assistance of Gianna and Pam to help me find the software before the divorce papers were served.

There was no way I could have known that three months into it, Pam, that scandalous traitor, would have started sleeping with him!

With nothing left to do but continue to play the role of the naïve wife, I kept things business as usual as it pertained to Pam, even though it was killing me inside.

One major rule that kept me from losing it was to avoid thinking about it. Thinking would have ruined my plans and my plans were all I had left.

A bout of dizziness flooded in and I clutched the kitchen

sink to keep myself steady. I thought I was going to throw up, but movements outside my kitchen window caught my attention.

The kids were playing, laughing, and chasing Gianna.

Despite her insistence on not using dirt in the reenactment of taking down the evil queen, her requests were completely disregarded.

Dirt bounced off her clothes and into the air while she ducked and dodged the angry three girl mob.

The sight brought me back to joy and peace, and I was calm when I spoke again.

"Did you tell Elijah that I was searching for the software?"

Pam actually sounded shocked. "God no! I would never betray you like that."

I knew she hadn't. Besides, there was no evidence to the contrary, but I still wanted to hear her say it.

"Oh, that's right. How could I forget? You're my loyal cousin, always looking out for my best interests."

"I mean it! I even tried to help you. Sometimes when Elijah came over, I would search through his things when he would go take a shower or step outside, hoping I would find something."

Pam's words baffled me.

All throughout high school, she'd continuously made honor roll and received awards based on her intelligence. I never understood how she lagged this far behind with common sense.

"Are you really doing this right now? Justifying not keeping your legs shut because you were helping me? How fucking dare you!"

"No," she sniffled. "I didn't mean it that way. I know what I did was wrong, but I would never tell him you were on to him. Bree, I truly never thought this would happen."

"You know what I never thought would happen? That I

would find my cousin, laughing and flirting her heart out, wearing the yellow dress that I bought her no less, sitting across from my husband because they were having an affair! You are a despicable bitch, and I will never forgive you for this."

"Bree, please." Were the last words I heard before ending the call.

My doorbell rang, and I went to open it, collecting the pizza from the delivery guy.

I noticed Hilary outside; her ass high in the air as she did some gardening around her mailbox.

As if she could sense my eyes on her, she turned and gave me a wave.

I closed the door as if I didn't even see her.

After calling everyone inside, we enjoyed a large pizza with everything.

Well, mine, Gianna's and the handcuffs pizza had everything. Ariel removed all her topping and just ate the bread and cheese.

I've tried to get her a plain cheese pizza in the past, but she says it tastes better when she removes the toppings.

Go figure.

Before long, Gianna and the twins left, and Grayson and Zoey were arriving home from school.

I was deciding on what to make for dinner when my phone rung, for the hundredth time that day. I'd now gotten sick of my ring tone and would change it to something else as soon as this call was over.

Hmm, that's odd, I don't know this number.

I almost let it go to voicemail, but I didn't get many telemarketer calls, so curiosity won out and I answered.

"Hello, this is a prepaid, collect call from," the audio recording paused and then I heard Elijah say his name before the robotic voice picked up from where it left off. "an inmate at Brunson County Jail. This call is subject to recording and monitoring. To accept charges, press one. To refuse charges, press two."

What the hell? Elijah was in jail?

Shifting the phone away from my ear, I focused my attention on the digital keypad and took several seconds before I finally reached a decision and pressed my chosen number.

Day 8

SATURDAY

12:43 PM

I was in no rush to get Elijah out of jail.

As a matter of fact, even though he called me in a suitable time frame to get him out yesterday, I waited until this morning.

A night in jail would do great things for that temper of his.

After I accepted the call yesterday. The only information Elijah would divulge was that he got into a fight with a *"mendacious asshole at work"*, his words, not mine.

My assumption was that it had to be related to one of his clients, given that the football players Elijah represented often had short fuses.

Turns out I was mistaken.

Shortly after we hung up, Evelyn called me from Elijah's job, wanting to inform me he had been arrested. I pretended I hadn't just spoken with him to gain more insight.

And what does she tell me?

That the mendacious asshole Elijah had gotten into a fight with was none other than his best friend.

However, even though Elijah instigated it, according to witnesses, Ryan threw the first punch. Therefore, they were both arrested.

Oh, shit.

Had Elijah learned of my affair with Ryan? Or had something concerning a client caused this outburst?

Arguments over work issues had ensued between Ryan and Elijah before, although never to this extent.

Regardless, I couldn't help but smile and hoped that Ryan beat his ass.

And, now having no one else, Elijah needed me to bail him out of jail.

How do you like that?

I giggled as I enjoyed my morning coffee because I didn't care how urgent this was. I would take my sweet time.

After finishing my coffee, I got the kids ready and dropped them off.

Once I had made it back to my humble abode, I was met with the task of selecting an outfit, and the fact that I couldn't make a choice resulted in a longer-than-anticipated period of deliberation.

Naturally, I gave up and decided that relaxing in front of the TV with a fruit bowl while I watched my favorite morning talk show would ultimately help me decide.

Two hours later, I was now in route to the county jail. Driving the speed limit, of course, and taking in the scenery.

The trees were lovely this time of year.

I'd called Ryan a few times to make sure he got out safely, and at first I received no answer.

Eventually, though, he texted he was okay and would call me later.

Parking in a spot near the front of the jail. I went inside and gave all the necessary paperwork for processing.

After my part was done, I went back to my car, pulled toward the front of the building, and waited.

Ah, there he is.

Exiting the building in a rush was an irritated Elijah, and

his face was in a permanent scowl. The button-down shirt he wore was torn at the arm and... *is that blood on his collar?*

It must have been, because now that he was closer, I could see that what I thought was a scowl was a slightly swollen lip and a bruised eye.

Way to go, Ryan.

But then I mentally retracted, because what if Ryan looked worse?

Opening the car door, Elijah got in and sat there, like a king waiting to be chauffeured around.

No "hello", no "thank you," or "how's your day, Bree?" Such poor treatment after I practically rushed down here to get him!

"Umm, you're welcome," I said.

I wouldn't move this car until he acknowledged me.

When Elijah spoke, his voice sounded hoarse.

"You left me in that hellhole for way longer than you needed to, and you want me to say thank you and ask about your day?"

There it was. He just needed to yell a bit. Maybe his voice sounded hoarse because he hadn't used it all night.

"It would be nice," I retorted. "Considering the way things were the last time I saw you, I shouldn't be here at all."

He looked at me. The swollen features combined with his enraged expression making me want to laugh. However, I held my composure.

In his lap sat a few sheets of paper that were stapled together. I assumed they were details that addressed the conditions of his release and when he should return for his court date.

I tried not to stare.

Who was I kidding? I totally tried to sneak a peek, but the only thing I saw was the line that read "No contact stipulation" before he flipped it over.

Asshole.

Considering his predicament, that would be tough. If he could have no contact with, or be around, Ryan, how was he going to go to work?

Sucks to be him.

"Just drive," Elijah snapped, straightening in his chair and pulling his seatbelt on.

It may not have been the type of acknowledgement I wanted, but it would have to do.

Putting the car in drive, and pulled off, not sure where to go. He wasn't staying at the house, secret divorce pending or not, and I wasn't supposed to know about his condo.

"Where should I take you? Pam's?"

I glanced over just in time to see him roll his eyes. Or maybe he was simply blinking. It was hard to tell with the way the swollen eye lagged.

He was staring straight ahead and the bad eye was the one closest to my side, so deciphering his expressions was a challenge.

"You can drop me off at my friends. He lives over on 3rd."

There was no friend. Elijah was going to his condo and with the view and first class amenities of that place, I wanted to go to his condo too, without him, of course.

I was in such a good mood.

I signaled a right turn to get onto the highway. Traffic was light, and the day was overcast again. Looks like we were in for more rain.

"Why did you and Ryan get into a fight?" I asked.

Elijah looked at me, surprised. Or it could have been a glare. That damn eye was confusing me.

"How do you know about that?"

"Mrs. Evelyn called. She thought I should know that you had been arrested so that I would expect your call and could make arrangements to come get you. Were you seriously not going to tell me why I was picking you up from jail?"

"I don't think it is important."

"You don't think the reason you got into a fight with your best friend is important? You and Ryan have been friends forever!"

"He is an asshole that I am not interested in talking about."

No, you're the asshole.

"At least tell me what he did?"

He remained silent for such an extended period that I doubted he would respond.

"Elijah," I repeated, reminding myself of the day Zoey sat in that same spot, ignoring me in the exact same way. Eyes fixed out the window, arms crossed, and a look of annoyance on her face.

"He stole one of my clients," Elijah said, as if that should be enough to shut me up.

Come on, Elijah, you can lie better than that.

Ryan had been his best friend for over ten years and had worked together for just as long. Clients had never incited an actual fist fight. Why would they now?

"A client. That's it?" I said unconvinced. "I'm sure there has to be more to it than that?"

"It isn't," Elijah said, keeping it short.

I wondered how the fight transpired. Who said what? Who did what?

My phone began vibrating on the flat surface I store it on near the gearshift. I glanced down in time to see "R calling" on the display.

Oh no!

Casually, I turned the phone over so that it was facedown. I wasn't sure if Elijah saw the caller ID, but I did not like the way he narrowed his eyes at me.

"Who was that?"

I gave him attitude.

"Why? It was only a friend."

"You could have answered it."

"I didn't want to. I will call her back once I drop you off."

The answer seemed to suit him, and he turned his focus forward again.

I felt a rush of relief wash over me, followed by annoyance. Why should it matter that I was having an affair with his best friend after he slept with my cousin?

It's not the time.

Keeping my sights set on getting some answers, I said, "It makes no sense. Why would you fight Ryan? Any issue the two of you had, I am sure it could have been easily settled."

"Not this one. He crossed the line."

"What line?" I pushed.

At this point, I'd figured it out, but it would be more satisfying if Elijah told me.

Plus, it would look suspicious if I didn't question him. We had been friends with Ryan since college. I had to try to mend the fences between the two of them. Even if I didn't give a shit.

"I said drop it, Bree."

I continued on like I didn't hear him, shaking my head.

"That doesn't sound like Ryan. He's always been a good guy."

"He's not."

"He's your best friend and cares about you. Maybe you should give him a chance to explain."

"I don't need any explanations from him," Elijah said, not wavering in the least.

"Well, I'd like to give him the benefit of the doubt. You should too."

Elijah faced me again.

"You know what I am wondering? Why does it sound like

you are taking his side over mine?" There was a long pause before he added. "Is there something going on between the two of you?"

Man, did he flip the tables quick.

I glared at him before fixing my eyes back on the road. "You slept with my cousin, so now I must be sleeping with your best friend, huh? Whatever, Elijah." I stated with irritation.

"You didn't answer the question."

"And I'm not going to. It's a ridiculous question."

Elijah rolled down the window slightly, took a deep breath, and let his head fall against the headrest, signaling the conversation was over.

There was no way I could ask him anything. Driving 75mph on the highway, with the wind pouring in, was deafening and prevented any question I asked from being heard.

We drove another few miles with the pounding wind as our soundtrack until I took the appropriate exit.

After making a right turn to put me in the direction of 3rd street, I said, "Which way do I turn once I get to 3rd?"

"Left. The condos are called The Gables."

I nodded. "What friend lives there?"

"Is this twenty fucking questions?" Elijah snapped. "I have had a rough evening and morning. All I want is to do is sit back and watch TV."

I was tiring of his ungrateful attitude. So what if I was only poaching him for information? He didn't know that!

For all he knew, I was still his faithful wife, oblivious to his plans.

It seemed like forever ago, but every time I recounted our years together, I didn't remember him being this rude.

True, we argued here and there like any couple, but nothing like this.

As a matter of fact, he was probably kinder. Since he was

cheating, he often played Mr. nice guy, bringing home roses, random gifts and pretending to care in an effort to beguile me with his charms.

Nowadays, he was constantly behaving like an audacious jerk.

It's disturbing that despite being his wife and the mother of his children, he no longer offered me any level of respect. It's as if any consideration for me vanished once he decided to move on.

Maybe I should pull this car over and let him walk the rest of the way, but then I'd be creating more problems.

No, I would take him to his condo and let him sit down in front of his precious TV, especially since I just remembered that I broke it.

He still had no idea. If he thought things couldn't get worse, he was in for a rude awakening.

I dropped Elijah off in front of the entrance to the condos and watched him walk inside. Neither of us said goodbye, and me remaining silent as he got out and slammed the door did nothing to lessen his anger.

He walked briskly, balling up the papers with his court information and throwing it into a nearby trashcan.

In his defense, he may have been yelling at me, but I wasn't the real reason for his frustrations. The missing software was.

And what did that have to do with the fight at his job?

You see, my husband thought that he had been double-crossed by his best friend and business partner, Ryan.

Yup, they'd struck up a deal with an investor for my software and neither man knew that I was aware of the secret business transaction.

However, now that the software was missing, who would Elijah blame for its disappearance?

Certainly not me.

I couldn't have known he had a safe in his office and even if I did, how would I know the combination?

Elijah only entrusted one person with that information, and it was Ryan.

My Ryan, the man that said he loved me. Did he love me? Why would he swindle me if he did?

Only Ryan could answer those questions, and I had yet to speak to him.

No worries, though.

In the meantime, let's see how the two best friends handled being pitted against each other. That software was worth millions, and I didn't see Elijah taking this sitting down.

His greed was far too powerful.

Elijah had become like a pirate on a ship that would do anything to protect his treasure, and I planned to burn the whole fucking ship down.

Two birds, one stone.

Day 9

SUNDAY
12:17 PM

"First, he sleeps with Pam and now you had to bail him out of jail for fighting Ryan?"

Gianna put the glass of water to her lips and took a long sip.

I'm certain the gesture had nothing to do with thirst and everything to do with Gianna trying not to say what she was thinking.

There was no doubt that I had Gianna's support, and that she felt for what I was going through, but I also knew drama TV was her guilty pleasure and even though her eyes are sympathetic, there is a small upward tug at her lips.

"Gianna, I remind you again that my life is not, emphasis on the not, one of your drama shows," I said pointedly.

"But isn't it?!" she exclaimed. "I mean, you know I love you to bits, but damn! This is straight off an episode of the dark chronicles of housewives or some shit."

My phone buzzed in my pocket, and I resisted checking it. More than likely it was Ryan, but I hadn't answered his calls since yesterday. I was no longer sure what I wanted to say.

His betrayal had come to a head, and I hadn't determined my next move. One thing was for sure, I couldn't let my emotions run the conversation.

If that happened, all of my responses would be based on agitation and hurt. That certainly wouldn't do.

"True," I said to Gianna, my eyes downcast. "My life is like a show, a horror show."

She reached to grab my hand. At the same time, a kid screamed across the room. Both Gianna and I looked over to the dessert area where the shriek had come from, but thankfully didn't see our kids.

We were at an indoor playground, giving Ariel and the handcuffs a fun outing to burn off some of their energy.

However, I had a sneaky suspicion being around other kids only recharged them. Even running them around outside in the sun didn't seem to help. I swore these kids today were solar powered.

After a few minutes of searching, we located our kids taking turns, swinging on a long rope and jumping off into a giant pool of foam.

"He took my ice cream," the little girl shouted, drawing our attention back to the line of kids by the dessert stand. She was pointing an accusatory finger at a boy holding an ice cream cone.

He stuck out his tongue at her and the girl screamed again, this time stomping her feet dramatically.

A woman, who must have been the girl's mother, rushed over, cutting her eyes at the boy and putting her arm around the girl.

The woman diffused the situation by offering the girl either another ice cream or something much better, because suddenly the girl wiped her tears away and smiled gleefully.

"She should have decked him," Gianna said.

We'd lost interest in the dessert stand drama, because again, it wasn't our kids.

Although, I imagine the outcome may have been slightly

different if it were. The boy would have been wearing the ice cream and maybe a few other items.

Ariel had a temper like her father. I was trying to ensure that she learned proper ways to diffuse it, but only time would tell.

Our current dilemma was her biting or scratching the kids at daycare that grabbed toys before she could get to them.

None of the punishments I enforced had completely eliminated the problem, but things had definitely gotten better, since I threatened to take some of her princess tutu's away.

She may have been too young to spell the word, but the girl loved fashion.

"Back to you," Gianna said. Giving my hand a comforting squeeze. "Fuck Elijah! You don't need that Pezzo di merda!" Her Italian accent was heavy, and she waved a dismissive hand. "You're better off without him anyway. The question is, did you find the software?"

"No, I haven't," I said with a straight face.

I'd decided not to share my findings with Gianna to avoid any potential future complications.

Gianna let out a low whistle. "So, what are you going to do? It's basically over. You have around six days before you get those divorce papers."

"I'm not going to do anything." I'd already done plenty. "He can serve me with the papers at this point. I have no fight left."

An odd feeling washed over me.

It felt like exhaustion and sorrow. I only made the comment because it sounded good and fit into the character I was currently showing Gianna, but was it true? Was there no more fight left in me?

I'd been with Elijah for fourteen years. That was a long time to endure as much as I had while raising kids. I actually wanted this to be over. Needed it to be over, in fact.

I had my software, and Elijah and Ryan were at odds. Their friendship wouldn't likely survive their greed. I could exit quietly.

What more could I do? What more did I want?

And in that precise moment, I realized the answer. Nothing.

All I wanted was my peace and sanity. This whole charade had turned my world dark. It was time to return to the light.

A neon sign on the wall toward the front door caught my eye.

Kids eat free on Sunday.

But the only words that were lit up were Free and Sunday.

To most people, that meant the sign wasn't working properly, but for me, it was confirmation. Divine intervention, if you will. Today was Sunday, the day of rest for many. What better day to end this mess?

"I have to go to the bathroom," I suddenly said to Gianna. "Will you keep an eye on Ariel for me?"

"Do you even have to ask that?" she said.

I knew I didn't, but it felt like the polite thing to do.

Giving Gianna a grateful smile, I headed in the direction of the bathroom, detouring at the last second to go toward the game section, where I wedged myself between two arcade machines.

Retrieving my phone, I texted Elijah that we needed to talk and for him to meet me at nine this evening.

At the last second, I added the name of a public place. I didn't want him coming to the house. I'd hate for a fight to start up in front of the kids.

Later, I would text Ryan asking if we could meet tomorrow night.

I wasn't going to tell him that I knew he and Elijah had plans to sell my software together. I wouldn't even ask if he ever really loved me, or wonder if I ever could have really loved him.

None of it mattered anymore and nothing he could say would justify what he did.

I'd cry, laying the waterworks on heavy, like this was the hardest decision of my life, when in fact, I'd be relieved. I was tired of playing games.

Thereafter, I would simply tell Ryan that our affair was over, because I needed to focus on my children.

Which, now that I think about it, wasn't a complete lie.

Before I could put my phone away, it beeped with a response from Elijah.

Elijah: That's fine. Bring the rest of my ties.

I wanted to scream. I'd never met a more narcissistic human being. Thank God I was about to be officially done with him.

Locating my composure, I tucked my phone back into my pocket and rejoined Gianna, pleasantly surprised to find that Ariel and the handcuffs were at the table as well, asking for food.

I guess it was time for lunch and since I now felt like celebrating, may as well get dessert too.

7:32 PM

"Your little game is over, Russ. I know you were the one who kidnapped Johnny."

"I... I didn't kidnap anyone," Russ said.

"Oh yeah," Linda replied, "So why are you holding the bag with the money from the ransom?"

Russ glanced down at the bag.

The bag that the police had marked to help catch the suspect responsible for kidnapping the judge's son, Johnny.

However, Russ had slipped from their grasp and escaped with the money and still hadn't returned the kid.

Fortunately for the parents, they'd hired Linda, a top rated private detective, to work the case. She'd tracked down Russ in less than a day.

Russ clutched the bag to his chest, darted left, darted right, but found no way out. No way to escape what was coming to him. He was going to jail.

"You can't run," Linda said, pointing the gun at him. "I've caught you red-handed. Turn yourself in and this will go a lot smoother."

I stood beside my bed, gripping the towel in my hand, watching one of my all-time favorite black and white movies.

The towel should have been folded and placed into a neat stack with the others. Instead, it had become a source of comfort that I held tightly to ease my apprehension.

Would Joe escape? Could Linda get him to give up the location of the child?

I already knew the answer, of course, but every time I watched this movie was like the first time. Justice was always served.

I began folding the towels again by the time the cops arrived, shoving Russ into the back of the police car.

Thanks to Linda's heroic efforts, little Johnny was safely found, and another crisis was averted.

"Mommy, I don't feel well," Ariel said, walking into my room. She was dragging her favorite pink blanket in one hand and her bear, Barney, with the wonky eye in the other.

That thing creeped me out. My mom gifted it to her as a baby, and she loved it instantly.

However, one day, when the bear lost an eye during a rough play session between Ariel and Grayson, he was rushed to mommy the medic, for repair.

I reattached the eye, but it was impossible to get it back to manufacturers' standards.

So now the bear always looked dizzy. Add in the fact that its eyes were so big, and glowed in the dark, and Barney became something you didn't want to see sitting in the dark.

I stopped folding towels and got down to Ariel's eye-level and touched her forehead. "What's wrong?"

"I feel like I am going to throw up."

Oh No!

I knew those hotdogs we had for dinner tasted weird. I should have tossed them out and made some lasagna or something, but I was still in a happy mood and thought hotdogs and fries would be a simple, yummy meal for us all.

"I think I have to..." Ariel made a weird face. Her cheeks puffed out and her eyes widened.

She dropped Barney and the blanket onto the floor and rushed toward the bathroom. I chased behind her, swooping her up into my arms in an attempt to fast track her to her destination.

Sadly, we didn't make it. After setting one foot inside the bathroom, vomit spewed everywhere.

And I mean everywhere: the wall, the counter, the cabinet and possibly even the ceiling.

Ariel was retching uncontrollably, tears streaming down her face, and thrashing about in my arms, while I frantically searched for a clean area on the floor where I could set her down.

It was unexpected, but the toilet turned out to be the ideal spot to put her. I closed the lid and sat her on top, mentally willing her not to also have a bout of diarrhea.

Surprisingly, sitting Ariel on the toilet proved to be beneficial for me because it made the task of cleaning up her vomit much more manageable.

Instead of having to deal with multiple small, sticky splatters of half-digested food everywhere, I only had to clean up one enormous pile.

"Mommy?" Ariel whispered.

"Yes, sweetie."

"Can you get Barney for me?"

"Oh, honey," I said, looking around at the destroyed bathroom, then back at Ariel. Strings of puke dripped down her chin and a few tiny chunks were stuck to the corners of her mouth. Her clothes and hair that she was currently touching was an absolute mess. "You don't want Barney getting vomit all over him, do you?"

Ariel nodded and cried. "Barney makes me happy."

I hated to see her cry, especially when she was sick. She looked even smaller and frailer during those instances.

"I'll tell you what," I said, coming closer to take Ariel's hand and help her off the toilet.

In the process, I almost slipped on a tiny puddle of vomit and shuddered. Lifting my bare foot, I wiped it off on a small nearby area rug.

That's it! This entire bathroom would need to be demolished.

"Let's get you cleaned up. Then I will tuck you and Barney back into bed. How does that sound?"

I guided Ariel out of the bathroom.

"Good, but can we hurry? Barney is afraid of being alone, and I don't want anything to scare him."

With those eyes of his, Barney was the one doing all the scaring, but all I said was, "Sure, we can. Are you feeling better?"

"Yes, I do,"

Ariel gave me a little smile, and that made me feel better.

Even with her face all sticky and gross, she was still adorable. Kids bounced back so quick.

When I got sick, it took seven to ten business days to improve, longer during the holidays.

I cleaned her up, and within twenty minutes, Ariel and crazy eyes were back in bed.

Returning to the kids' bathroom, I looked around at the mess that awaited me.

Gross! There was already a stench settling in.

This was going to take forever to clean.

Collecting the towels and bathroom rugs, I dropped them off in the laundry room, where I also collected a bucket, gloves, disinfectant cleanser, and a roll of paper towels.

When I got back to the bathroom, Grayson was standing in front of the bathroom door, his hand on his stomach, his eyes squinting from the light.

I assumed he didn't go into the bathroom because it was a current wasteland, but from the look on his face, he would need a toilet, too.

"Mom, I don't feel so good," he squeaked, confirming my suspicions.

Wordlessly, I pointed in the direction of my bathroom. "Use mine. I am about to clean this one up."

Grayson dragged himself away, and I picked up the bucket, entering the war zone.

Not even ten minutes later, another kid sounded off behind me, hovering around the bathroom entrance.

"Mom?"

It was Zoey, displaying the same painful expression, clutching her stomach and looking for me to make it all better.

I guess no matter how old kids got, when they were sick, it was mommy to the rescue.

"Use the bathroom downstairs," I said. "Grayson is in the other and I am cleaning this one. I will come check on you in a minute."

Now all the bathrooms in the house were occupied. It was going to be a long night.

Needless to say I spent two hours thoroughly cleaning all of the bathrooms, giving medicines and forehead kisses.

I collapsed onto my bed, exhausted and achy with the smell of regurgitated food still lingering in my nostrils.

I desperately needed a shower, but all I really wanted to do was sleep. The trouble was, I felt like there was something I was supposed to be doing.

What was it?

The thought nagged at the back of my mind, unable to be recovered because I felt spacey, like my head was buried in the clouds.

But when my stomach began to cramp and the overwhelming feeling of fluid rushed up my chest and threatened to project from my mouth, I rolled over in bed and buried my head in the trashcan.

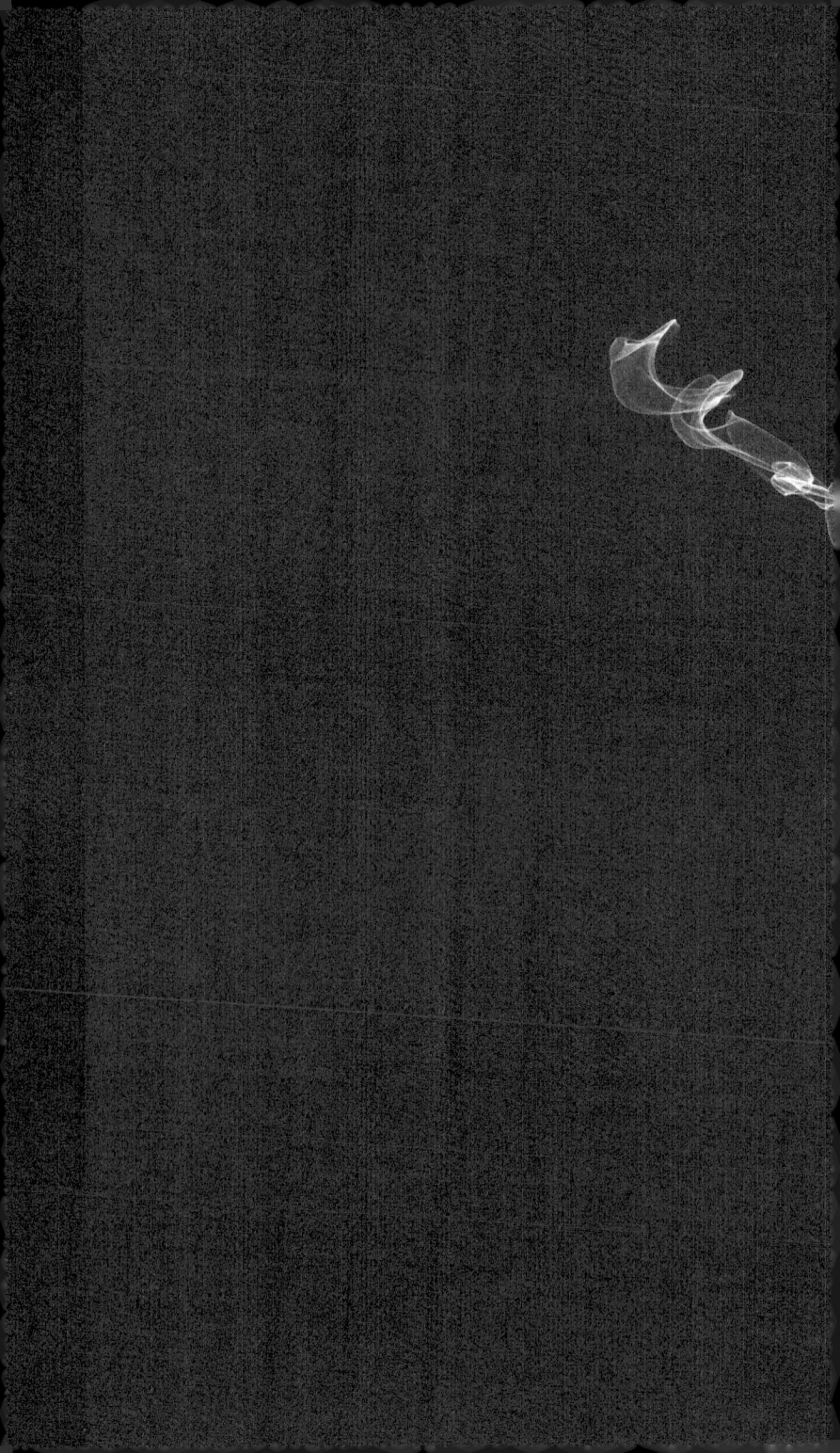

Day 10

MONDAY
12:03 PM

It was as if last night had never happened, at least for the kids.

As for me, I was still fighting fatigue and dehydration. It appeared that the sickness was an isolated incident; the culprit being the hotdogs and not some virus going around.

Therefore, to make a long vomit-filled story short, the children were at their appropriate learning centers happy and healthy and my morning had been productive.

I'd gathered boxes from the attic and filled them with Elijah's belongings.

The bedroom and bathroom were officially Elijah free, and four boxes stuffed with his things were stacked near the front door.

There was still a lot he would need to pack, but at least now I'd got the ball rolling.

I strolled through the hallway of my two-story home, traveling down memory lane to determine how choices of the past could affect the future.

As I approached each child's bedroom door, I took the time to pause and reflect as I sipped a cup of coffee.

In hindsight, my drink may have been an irresponsible choice since I was still dehydrated from my brush with death last night, but I liked to live dangerously.

My fingers brushed across the knob of Ariel's door.

My happy, rambunctious fire storm.

How would all my choices affect her? Would she grow up to be the strong yet sophisticated woman I hoped she would? Putting her unique and courageous personality to good use by standing up for the little guy?

Then there was Grayson.

I stopped in front of his bedroom. The door was always open. It was as if it were an invitation for the world.

Come see me! Chat with me! You are welcome anytime!

Had Elijah's constant rejections scarred his loving spirit? Would he grow up and seek approval from others to determine his self worth? Or could my next decision cement his confidence and protect his heart?

And Zoey.

Her door not only shut, but... I twisted the knob... locked, as I suspected.

Would my moody, soft-spoken girl turn into a vengeful woman, like her mother? Keeping everyone at arm's length in order to protect herself?

Was there something I could do about that? Or would nature simply outweigh nurture as it pertained to her? Leaving me powerless to do anything but love her the way she was.

Moving past the kids' bedrooms, I continued to roam the hallway, my gaze taking in the photos that lined the wall.

There were dozens of them, laid out in a way that explained the journey of our family.

I touched the edge of the first photo, covering my finger tip with a thin layer of dust. It was Elijah and me in college. Our entire world was ahead of us, and we had no idea what a ride it would be.

I continued on to the next, watching my world unfold through the still images.

Ryan and Pam suddenly appearing in the photos as the

four of us became our own family, but eventually they faded into the background.

College was ending and Zoey took up center stage in our world.

Were they happy years? Or destructive ones?

I pressed on.

Zoey aging, growing, learning from two adults that were still, in ways, children themselves.

Suddenly Grayson is in the picture, crawling behind his big sister, running in the park with his father, proudly displaying his yellow belt from karate.

Elijah's smile faltering as the photos progress and mine growing larger to compensate and cover up the secrets.

"There isn't a smile big enough to hide it all, Bree," I said aloud to my past self.

And then Ariel joined us on the journey. My beautiful baby girl. The one that changed me.

After her, I saw the world in a new light. Understood the difference between love and lust, heaven and hell, hope and hopeless.

For my entire marriage, I had existed on the wrong side and although I didn't see it then, I could see it now.

Elijah barely smiled in the most recent photos and his hands no longer embraced me.

Instead, those hands held the kids, then awards from his job, eventually they were no longer visible because they were stuffed in his pockets and as I stand in front of the final few pictures, Elijah nor his hands are there at all.

Just me and the kids.

He was done pretending and so was I. Delusions didn't make dreams come true, determination did.

Done with reminiscing and riding the wave of emotions, I glanced up at the clock on the wall.

Like the photos, it too could use a serious dusting, but it would have to wait until another day.

Elijah had texted me earlier, he was due to be here in fifteen minutes, and I needed to get dressed.

2:15 PM

The sound of Elijah's car pulling into the driveway over an hour after he was supposed to arrive didn't upset me.

On the contrary, I was grateful to have more time to enjoy the silence.

He opened the front door, with the key that he refused to return, and knocked over his box of things I'd stacked there.

"Shit," he said, pushing the door closed and bending over to repack the items that had fallen out.

His ties, underwear, shoes and colognes formed a giant pile near his feet.

I watched him from the couch while drinking a bottle of water, finally addressing my dehydration issue.

"You're just going to sit there?" he asked, reaching out to catch a bottle of cologne as it rolled across the floor.

The act caused him to drop some ties and shirts he was holding, and he cursed again.

Finally dumping everything into the box. He let out a long sigh and crossed his arms.

He was wearing black gym shorts and an old white t-shirt with the sleeves cut off.

I rolled my eyes. He must have just come from the gym.

I remember a time when seeing him, all bulk and sweaty from working out, was a turn on. Now, the thought made me nauseated.

"What would you have me do?" I asked, responding to his question about me not coming over to assist.

"You could help. Or you could have never put the boxes there in the first place."

When I didn't respond. Elijah said, "What happened to you last night? I waited for over two hours."

"The kids and I were sick."

Elijah moved on to his next question, not interested in the health of me or his children.

"And you couldn't even answer your cellphone? I called you a hundred times."

Lies! You only called once.

Letting the thought remain in my head. I pushed my agitation aside and said, "I'm sure the football game kept you busy in my absence."

I knew Elijah. There was no way he would see a football game playing on TV and not finish it. Football was his life. I would bet anything that he kept his ass planted in that chair until the game was over and barely thought about me.

Elijah hesitated and then said, "That's not the point. I could have watched the game somewhere else."

He meant with someone else, and that someone was likely the new woman he was banging.

I put my bottle of water down and walked over to him. This was either going to be smooth or rough.

Clearing my throat, I mentally crossed my fingers that it would go smoothly.

"I'll make this short," I said. "I think that our time together has run its course."

My confused husband's brows shot up. "What do you mean it's run its course?" Elijah asked.

Rough it is.

There was no need for him to make this difficult, but of course he would, even though he wanted this!

The papers from his divorce attorney were probably already en route to me. Yet, he wanted to play dumb.

I was cutting him loose, letting the bird fly free. What was with the dumb question? He knew we were done.

"Elijah," I said, as if I were talking to one of my children. "This has been a long time coming. All we do is fight."

"That's because you nag me all the damn time."

"You are my husband. Asking you where you are going or when you are coming home is not nagging!"

"Yeah, it is!" he shouted back. "I'm not a child. I don't need to tell you anything. You are my wife, not my mother."

That pissed me off and suddenly, we were both yelling and cursing at each other like two insane people on the street, tossing out insults like they were going out of style.

He said I wasn't good in bed. I said I am when I have a partner that knows what he is doing.

Then he said I'm too big to be sexy, and I told him I definitely knew a few men that would beg to differ.

It was a pointless and vicious cycle because somehow we ended up right back at him claiming I thought I was his mother.

"Oh, I'm acting like your mother, huh? Well, where are these complaints when I cook you dinner? Wash your clothes? Or run errands for you? You don't seem to have much to say then."

He pointed a finger at me.

"See!" He shouted. "You are always trying to flip my words. A wife is supposed to do those things, but I don't need to report back to you."

There was so much wrong with what he said, I didn't know where to begin.

I crossed my arms, uncrossed them, then put my hands on my hips, in an effort to keep them busy because they were itching to be wrapped around his neck.

"Explain the cheating then," I spat.

I was in way too deep and I wanted answers.

"What cheating?" Elijah said with a straight face.

I held up my hand, lowering a finger as I listed them.

"The hairstylist, Sarah, Julia, that mom at Zoeys school, Pam," I said, saving my middle finger for the last one.

Elijah had the nerve to chuckle. "You are talking about things in the past. I am not cheating now."

"You know what?" I said, lifting my hands in surrender. "It doesn't matter. Then, now, tomorrow, it's all the same."

He had demolished my wall of peace and drew me back into his unstable world, but I was hitting the emergency exit.

"It's not all the same," he said, taking a step toward me, "If I am trying to win you back."

What the hell was happening?

"Elijah, I'm not interested in continuing anything with you."

He stepped closer yet again, and I took a step back.

"Stop," I warned, reaching into my back pocket to ensure I had my cellphone.

I didn't need to pull it out because thankfully Elijah stopped moving, but he still continued to speak his madness.

"Bree, come on, we have been together for fourteen years. We have three beautiful kids. I know you don't want to throw this all away."

Was I dreaming?

Maybe I'd never woken up this morning.

"You threw all this away, not me," I replied.

"Now I'm trying to make up for it," he said with a shrug. "I do still love you."

Was this a pride thing? It had to be a pride thing. If not pride, then there was an angle.

But what was it?

I narrowed my eyes at him. "If you wanted to work it out with me, why have you been taking your stuff? You even asked me to bring your precious ties."

In case I needed to retrieve my phone quickly, I kept my hand near my back pocket.

"Bree," he said, smiling innocently. "It was only temporary. I figured I'd give you some space and then in a few weeks we could go to counseling or whatever you want and start over."

"We aren't starting over, Elijah."

"So the fact that I still love you means nothing?"

"You don't love me. You probably never have."

"You know that's not true. Besides, we are good together."

"When are we good together?" I said, crossing my arms.

I couldn't resist. I wanted to see what was up his sleeve.

"Most of the time we are," he said, clearly searching for these many examples of us being some great couple. He snapped his fingers. "Raising the kids for one."

Ha! I'd been doing that practically alone since I had them.

"Planning the annual events for my job," he continued.

Again, alone. And wasn't that more about him than us?

"And what about when you helped me create that software for my clients, remember? We were even going to go into business together," he said, an odd glint in his eye.

And there it was!

That insufferable shithead wanted me to rebuild the software for him, since he didn't know where the original was. Well, Elijah could kiss my ass.

I nodded in the direction of his boxes that were now behind him, because he had taken a few steps in my direction. "You've overstayed your welcome."

Elijah's arms dropped to his side and his tone shifted to something cold that I didn't like. "You are being unreasonable, Bree."

I swallowed hard, and this time pulled my cellphone from my pocket.

"Take your boxes and go before I call the police," I warned.

Elijah faced away and kicked one box hard enough to make a hole. I jumped, but held my ground. He would not intimidate me.

With a slightly shaky finger, I pressed 9, 1, 1 on my phone and showed it to him. "Do I need to complete this call?"

For a second, he only stood there, contemplating his next move, but eventually, he gritted his teeth and said, "Fine. I need to get a few more of my things, but this conversation isn't over. You don't get to walk away from us."

Was he threatening me?

"For now, you can take the boxes. I think you should get the rest of your stuff on a different day when you are calmer."

Elijah's voice elevated again.

"Stop trying to run me! This is my house, and I will do what I want."

He snatched up one of his boxes and carried it outside, returning seconds later to get the other three.

Entering the house yet again, he stormed past me and went upstairs. I almost called out to stop him, but let him go. There was nothing left in the bedroom for him to pack.

However, he didn't go toward the bedroom; he went toward his office.

I sat on the stairs and patiently waited for him to return, hoping it would be soon. I wanted him gone.

Through the open front door, I saw a police car pull into the driveway.

Dammit, Elijah.

With all the screaming and arguing we were doing, I'll bet someone filed a noise complaint.

I stood, then walked to the open front door, staring out the screen door as they approached.

"I am so sorry, officers," I said, embarrassed. "We didn't mean to cause a scene. He is getting his things now and will be leaving."

"Ma'am, is Elijah Simmons home?"

I furrowed my brow, but before I could answer. Elijah called out from the top of the stairs.

"I'm Elijah Simmons. What's this about?"

"Sir, could you please come down?"

I noticed the officer's hand shift to rest on his weapon and an eerie feeling washed over me.

Elijah took the stairs cautiously. Eyeing me the whole way down.

This isn't my fault! I didn't call them.

"Officers, my wife sometimes gets beyond herself and—"

The officer cut him off, forcing him to turn around and, to my horror, cuffed his hands.

"Elijah Simmons," the officer said, "You are under arrest for the murder of Ryan Burton."

Day 11

TUESDAY
8:47 AM

I was smoking two cigarettes at a time. One in each hand. Shaking my leg back and forth, letting the enormity of this situation sink in.

This was an absolute mess.

Yesterday, neighbors witnessed Elijah being carted off by the police all the while screaming he hadn't killed Ryan and it took no time for the gossip to spread through the neighborhood like wildfire.

I even think the story of Ryan being found dead made the 6 o'clock news, and it took no time for people to put two and two together.

Since then, I'd been receiving the random drop-by from neighbors pretending to be concerned when they really wanted some information.

The only reason Gianna didn't hear about it was because, as usual, she was tending to her kids and barely talked to anyone in the neighborhood except me, but she was here now and making my anxiety worse.

"What in the all out hell," Gianna said. "Ryan is dead and Elijah is the killer."

I wasn't sure if it was a question, an acceptance or deep denial, but those words, along with a dry hello were the only things she'd said since she arrived ten minutes ago.

I'd dropped the kids off with my mom, because after all the commotion yesterday, I felt it was best that they skip school.

As soon as I returned home, I'd called Gianna and told her that Ryan had been found shot to death and that Elijah was the prime suspect.

Normally, I wouldn't have bothered her so early in the morning, but I needed the mental support.

However, now I wondered if I would have to get support for Gianna.

I took a long pull on the cigarette from my right hand, and when that didn't give me the mellow vibe I craved, I took a puff from the one in my left.

This was my fault. All my fault!

Had I pushed him too far? I knew Elijah was a greedy man with a bad temper, but did that mean disaster was inevitable?

"Give me one of those," Gianna said, snatching the cigarette from my right hand and taking a long pull of her own. After releasing a cloud of smoke, she began speaking Italian faster than I'd ever heard.

"What the hell are you saying?" I asked, lowering my cigarette to side-eye her.

She wasn't talking to me and no one else was in the room.

"I am praying for and cursing Elijah at the same time. If he is innocent, God help him, but if he is guilty, may he dance with the devil."

"So you're pleading for two things at once?"

"I got to cover all my bases here!" Gianna replied like it was a no-brainer.

"Oh," I said. The ash from the cigarette missing the tray and falling onto the table, courtesy of my trembling hand. "Carry on."

I went back to my inner thoughts, and Gianna went back to her two-sided prayer.

This was such a wild and unbelievable unfold of events. I was having trouble thinking about what I should do next.

Questions kept swimming around in my head and the anxiety of how all this would end had me on edge.

Would Elijah beat the charges? If he didn't, what did this mean long term? How would the kids handle it? And the biggest question of all. Was he guilty?

"Are they sure there wasn't some mistake?" Gianna asked, cutting into my thoughts.

One of her velcro rollers had come loose and was dangling at the end of her shoulder length hair.

My friend was in such shock when I called that she hurried right over, without taking out her rollers or changing from her pajamas.

I took a sip of my coffee before responding.

"I spoke to Elijah. During the interrogation, they said witnesses place him near the scene and they found the murder weapon."

"That doesn't necessarily mean it's him," Gianna offered. "That gun could belong to anybody."

"But it doesn't." I said quietly, "The gun is registered to Elijah. Has his prints on it and everything."

"Damn," Gianna said, staring straight ahead. "He's going to rot in jail."

Was he? And if so, how did I feel about that?

I mean, karma was a bitch, but damn.

I'd signed him up for spam accounts, made fraudulent charges to his credit cards and even put rat droppings in his food a few times.

But jail? A small room, complete with iron bars and no privacy attached to a life sentence for murder. That made me feel bad for the guy.

Before I could further process my thoughts, Gianna threw up her hands, cigarette ash falling to the kitchen floor.

"But why would he kill Ryan?! Ryan is such a nice guy and Elijah's best friend. None of this makes any sense."

It might make better sense to her if she knew that Ryan and Elijah were business partners on a deal for my software, but now that I had found and reclaimed the software without their knowledge, Elijah had become convinced that Ryan stole it from him to form his own deal.

However, I would not give her that insight.

"Why has Elijah done any of the things he has done?" I offered as explanation. "I don't think anyone knows that but Elijah."

"I guess you're right."

Gianna went back into her zone of disbelief while I checked my phone and turned a deaf ear to the sound of my doorbell ringing.

I didn't know who was at my door this early, could be a neighbor or a reporter, neither I wanted to have a heart-to-heart with.

There were more pressing issues on my mind. I was awaiting a call from Elijah's lawyer. As the cops hauled him off yesterday, he had repeatedly yelled that I contact an attorney named Gordon Bridges.

A quick search on the internet revealed that Mr. Bridges was a criminal defense attorney.

According to the website, Mr. Bridges had over fifteen years' experience defending the wrongfully accused and would "go above and beyond to vigorously fight your case."

The website's motto sounded promising. Still, I couldn't help but wonder, *why did Elijah already have a defense attorney picked out?*

It could be as simple as Mr. Bridges was one of the many people Elijah had networked with over the years.

Lord knows there were always stories about the football

players Elijah represented getting into trouble or being accused of crimes.

Yet, no matter what spin I put on it, red flags were raised.

"Do you think he did it?" Gianna asked.

She had put the cigarette down and was removing her hair rollers, placing them in a neat line on the table.

"No," I said honestly.

Elijah was a lot of things… but a murderer? I didn't think so. Despite that, the evidence begged to differ.

To add to the stress, because of his job with high-profile clients, the judge had already denied him bail, stating that Elijah was a flight risk.

Bridges planned to have Elijah surrender his passport and meet with the judge again, but that could take months.

"Are you going to tell the kids about it today?" Gianna asked.

"No, I am going to give it a little more time. Maybe he can beat the charges."

Gianna winced. "The murder weapon and witnesses? Sorry Bree, but if that's true, the only person Elijah is going to be tucking into their bed at night is his cellmate."

I took a few more puffs on the cigarette, then put it out, placing my forehead in my hands. Too much was happening too fast.

"I need to figure out what the kids are having for dinner," I said, suddenly sitting up. "I haven't been to the store yet and if I don't do it soon, there will be nothing left."

"Bree, it's nine in the morning," Gianna said carefully. "Dinner isn't for a long time, and I will help you figure something out."

I heard Gianna's words, but that's all they were, words.

They had no meaning, made no sense. I felt like I was spiraling.

There were three children in this house I needed to care for. I didn't have time for a murder case. Grayson had a doctor's appointment next week, for goodness' sakes!

"Zoey is probably going to need braces soon," I said, still consumed by future obligations. "And Grayson has all those soccer games. I need to look at the calendar and see how many we have to travel for. Ariel isn't great on long car rides, so I will have to ask my mom to keep her like I did last—"

"Hey!" Gianna said, waving a hand in front of my face. "None of that matters right now. You're losing it and that makes sense because I would be too, but everything is going to be fine. We have to take this one step at a time, alright? One step at a time."

I nodded and repeated her words, "One step at a time."

"That's right. And if Elijah is convicted, you can decide what you are going to do then. No decisions need to be made immediately."

It sounded like a solid plan and one that I could manage, but then Gianna's brow furrowed, and I feared something terrible.

"Are you still going to divorce him?" she asked.

"Huh?"

"You know, the divorce papers that he filed? Aren't they due in the next several days?"

"Oh wow, they are," I said. "I hadn't thought about that since all of this happened."

"Well, what are you going to do?"

I shook my head.

"One minute you tell me, don't worry and then you turn around and drop this big weight on me. What happened to no decision has to be made right now? I was kinda enjoying that idea."

Gianna laughed.

"I'm sorry, but this decision may not be able to wait. From what I gathered, he already has the ball in motion, so you are going to be served soon, like it or not."

I sighed and bit my lower lip. "Maybe I shouldn't sign them right away?"

Gianna's mouth fell open. "Are you considering staying with him?!"

"Yes... no... I don't know! How am I supposed to handle this? Just leave?"

"Pretty much," Gianna said without hesitation. "I mean, guilty or innocent Elijah is no longer your problem. He wanted out, so now he's out. Nothing changes because he got himself into some deep *merda*."

I didn't have to ask her what that word meant. She'd said the Italian word for shit in enough instances that I could point that word out in a lineup.

A line up? Was Elijah going to be put in a lineup? Had he already?

"This is all surreal, Gianna."

"It is, but I've got your back. Starting with dinner for the kids."

"You'd do that for me?" I asked, a bit stunned. "Even though you said the handcuffs can be absolute terrors at dinnertime?"

"Even though," Gianna said, appearing to momentarily reconsider, but then she shrugged and pushed on. "It is like herding cats with those two sometimes, but whatever, what's three more? And who knows, maybe your kids being over will actually calm mine down."

When it was time for dinner, Gianna's kids were far from typical.

When they were babies, they sat in their high chairs and accepted different varieties of food without fuss, but as they grew and became more independent, their stubborn attitudes set in.

They no longer wanted foods that touched, were too dry, too wet, of a certain color, or that resembled a certain shape. The list went on and on.

And if that weren't bad enough, they also spent most of their time playing instead of eating, dragging dinner out for two hours sometimes.

Once, after Gianna had set the table and stepped away to take a phone call, she returned to an empty table.

Apparently, the handcuffs didn't approve of the meal choice and hid it in the laundry room.

She'd punished, threatened, reasoned and even sent them to bed without dinner on rare occasion, but no response fixed their meal-time manners permanently.

Nonetheless, today was a weird day in my world. Maybe that would work out in Gianna's favor.

"I doubt my kids will make yours any better," I finally said. "But you can't retract now."

Gianna finger combed her hair into a ponytail, then twisted it into a knot on the top of her head before heading to the counter to pour herself a cup of coffee.

"It's fine," she said. "I'll even go pick up Zoey and Grayson from school and Ariel from daycare. That way, you won't have to deal with them until bedtime."

I placed my hand over my chest.

"Thank you, my gutsy friend. I owe you big time."

"No, you don't. This is me proving to you that everything will work out."

Maybe Gianna had some special powers I didn't know about, because suddenly my cell rung. The display announced a call from Attorney Bridges and it couldn't have happened at a better time.

I looked up at Gianna with a relieved smile and she said, "Told you so."

Stepping away to take the call in private, I felt silly for stressing about any of this in the first place.

Gianna was right. Everything would work out.

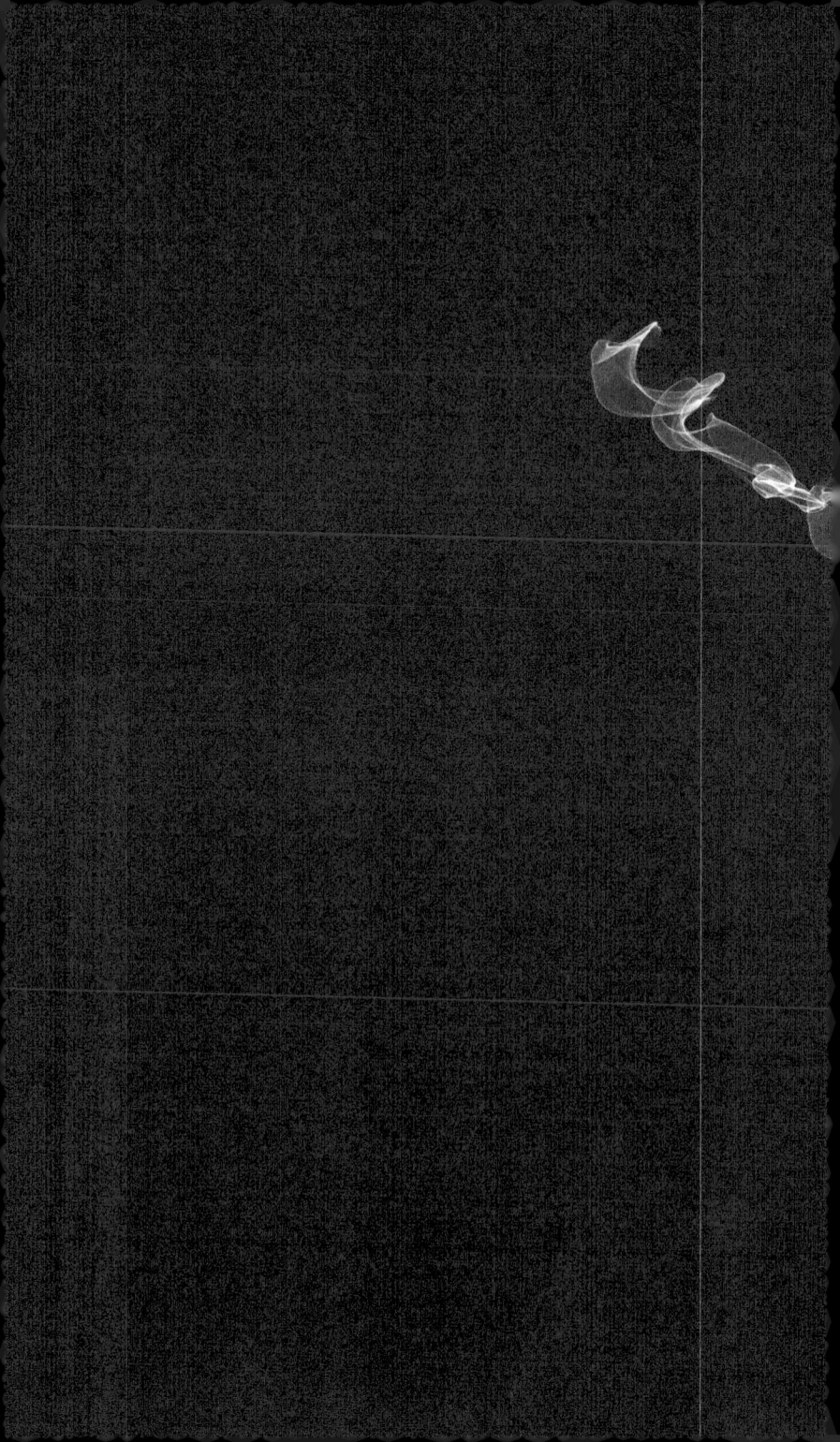

Day 12

WEDNESDAY
10:55 AM

Elijah and I had spoken to Bridges, separately of course, and according to the attorney, the evidence was going to be tough to beat.

Already he was considering tactics for Elijah to plead guilty so that they could get a deal, but Elijah wasn't hearing it.

"I did not kill him, so I won't say I did," Elijah had sworn to both me and the attorney.

But the evidence, oh the evidence, was telling a different story.

First, there was the murder weapon and witnesses.

Then the pile only grew once the fight that occurred between Elijah and Ryan at the office was added.

According to the law; it gave Elijah motive for the murder and made things appear premeditated.

I asked Bridges about the fight since Elijah would never come out and tell me himself, but neither would Bridges.

He claimed it fell under Attorney–client privilege, and must be kept confidential.

How do you like that?

As his wife, I can help retain the attorney, provide payments for his fees, but not know what they discussed? Sounded like a scam to me.

Yet, one beneficial thing came from all that legal mumbo jumbo.

As Elijah's spouse, I legally couldn't be compelled to testify against him. Didn't matter since I didn't know anything, but it was a relief to know that I wouldn't need to be on the stand swearing about it.

Anyway, that meant I was still in the dark about what really happened during the fight and Elijah's reasonings for starting at.

All the employees at Elijah's job claimed to not have heard the conversation between the two men.

Apparently, Elijah stormed into Ryan's office and closed the door.

However, once Jim, another agent, heard glass breaking and someone being slammed into the wall, the cops were called.

This was a mess.

Gianna offered to come over again, but I declined.

Talking to her was helpful, but this morning I needed my alone time.

My mom was going to keep the kids for the rest of this week and I had to gather the list of things the attorney needed.

I was upstairs in my bedroom, putting papers in an envelope, when I heard my doorbell.

"That better not be another neighbor, with good intentions," I grumbled.

People had stopped coming by around five yesterday afternoon. I was grateful, thinking it was all over. I hoped it wasn't starting up again.

I went down stairs annoyed and cursing myself for not installing one of those doorbell cameras everyone had nowadays.

As soon as things calmed down, that was going to be my first purchase.

I glanced through the side glass panel, and to my utter shock, saw Pam standing there.

She was wearing a gray and blue button up sweater over her teal scrubs, her arms wrapped around her body.

When she noticed me, she offered a warm smile.

Well, I'm already at rock bottom.

Opening the door, I allowed her inside.

"Hi," she murmured.

I turned on my heel and headed to the kitchen. She could either follow me or decide coming over wasn't a good idea and leave.

I was hoping for the latter, but she did the former.

Entering the kitchen, I went straight to the counter and poured myself a shot of gin.

The bottle was my saving grace last night when I couldn't stop my thoughts from moving too fast, and now was a suitable time for another.

Throwing back the shot, I didn't offer Pam anything to drink, or any additional conversation.

Despite that, she sat down, clasping her hands together.

I had no idea why she was nervous. Elijah was already in jail for murder. I didn't plan on joining him.

She's safe... for now.

"I heard about Ryan."

That brought my annoyance at her presence down several notches.

It suddenly occurred to me how others who knew him might take the news. Family, coworkers and old friends would be devastated.

Pam had known Ryan for as long as I did since we all attended college together. Naturally, his death would mean something to her.

"Yeah," I said. "It's horrible. How'd you hear about it?"

"The news. At first I didn't believe it, so I called Red Zone where they work... or worked," she muttered. "And Mrs. Evelyn confirmed it."

They.

I didn't like it. She was no longer a part of this family, no longer welcomed to speak about any of us on a familiar plane. But I said nothing, only continued to watch her.

Something was up. I knew my cousin.

The news of Ryan was not the only reason she came by.

With my eyes narrowed and shoulders tensed. I realized it may not have been a good idea to let her in. I was still too angry.

"I would have called to ask you about it, but..." Pam's voice trailed off, and I mentally warned her to tread carefully. But she switched the direction of the conversation entirely, toying with the button on her sweater. "They think Elijah did it."

I don't know if it was just me, but I heard skepticism in her tone.

"Maybe he did," I snapped.

I knew what she was thinking, that Elijah couldn't be a murderer. It didn't matter that I agreed with her. I resented the insinuation that I needed her input on this.

Broadcasting that she was familiar enough with Elijah to know what he was, and wasn't, capable of was a ballsy move.

"I'm not trying to make you angry, Bree. I came here to see how you were holding up."

"Just fine," I said, shifting away from her and pouring another drink.

It hurt to look at her.

Having loved and trusted her wholeheartedly, it was now necessary for me to disregard those feelings.

In order to cope with my emotions, I had to push them aside, ball them up and pretend they never existed until one day they no longer did.

Horns blowing outside redirected my attention from Pam. It was almost time for the mailman and I had better things to do.

"Well," I said, facing her again. "Thanks for coming by. You can show yourself out."

Pam didn't move. In fact, she straightened her shoulders and held her head high.

I released my hold on the shot glass and placed my hands on my hips. My cousin was about to face her own criminal charges for trespassing. If she didn't leave my house soon.

"I wanted to ask you something." When I remained quiet, Pam took that as an invitation to continue. "That day on the phone after you, uh... saw Elijah and us at Atlas, you mentioned the yellow dress that you bought me."

Releasing a long sigh, I rolled my eyes. Evidently, there was something significant that she felt compelled to share.

"And?" I spat.

"I wasn't wearing a yellow dress the day you found us at the restaurant. I was wearing a red one."

Without thought, laughter rose out of me. Is this what she wanted to say? That I remembered her fashion choices for that night incorrectly.

"Pam, I don't give a damn what you were wearing when you were caught out on a date with," I paused and pointed at myself. "my husband, you could have been naked for all I care and come to think about it, I'm sure later that night you would have been."

Despite my statement, Pam showed no regard and continued on like a woman that had no value for her life.

"How long had you known about us, Bree?"

Irritation was growing inside me at an alarming rate.

"I knew about you when I saw you. Don't you remember? I snatched you out of your chair and picked up a knife. An action I am leaning towards repeating."

"Just tell me the truth."

"The truth!" I shouted. "You want the truth? Well, here it is. I never should have let you into my house. After everything you did, you have the audacity to come here asking me ridiculous questions!"

"They are not ridiculous," Pam yelled back. "I wore that yellow dress on the first day Elijah and I started our..." she mumbled what sounded like affair, then pressed on. "That was months ago. I remember because there was an event at my job and I wanted to wear something that made me look nice."

She smiled as if she were revisiting the memory.

"Afterward, Dylan was supposed to meet me at Atlas and treat me to dinner." Her eyes dropped to her hands. "He never showed, and I was heartbroken. As I was leaving, I spotted Elijah sitting at the bar. He asked me what was wrong. We talked and things got out of hand after that."

"Boo fucking hoo," I said. "What's your point?"

Her eyes darted to mine.

"You knew about that night three months ago, just like you knew to show up the night you confronted us." Pam tilted her head and studied me. "But you were biding your time."

I crossed my arms. "And why would I do something like that?"

"Because you've done it before, in high school with Daisy Ramirez. I know you, Bree. You wait, you plan, and then you strike."

Ah, Daisy Ramirez.

The nemesis of my sophomore year and Carver High's resident mean girl.

Daisy lied and said that I cheated on a major project, when the truth was it was she who cheated.

Nevertheless, Daisy somehow planted all the evidence in my locker, and I received a failing grade for that assignment. Which as a result made me fail the class.

I had to attend summer school to make that up.

To say I was indignant about the way I had been treated was an understatement, but little lying Ramirez got what was coming to her.

The next school year, I befriended Daisy.

"No, I was no longer upset about that awful lie. It was water under the bridge," I'd told Daisy.

And she believed it, eventually welcoming me into her circle. And why wouldn't she?

I was smarter than her, so I gave her all the answers for the tests. I showed up at her house with cupcakes when she was sad and even helped her score a date with the hottest guy in school.

It is extremely unfortunate that, as the school year came to a close, pages of Daisy's diary were delivered anonymously to the members of the school board.

Shocking entries that revealed various misdeeds, such as orchestrating schemes against fellow students and engaging in inappropriate relationships with a teacher.

It was odd. I never saw Daisy again after that.

I wonder what happened to her?

Pam was awaiting my response, but again I didn't say a word. Often enough, she was off base with a lot of things.

"Why did you wait, Bree?" she asked quietly. "What did you plan this time?"

But she wasn't off base about this.

"You know where the door is," I announced, leaving the kitchen.

Dignifying Pam's suspicions with a response was something I would not do. She didn't deserve one, and the damage was done.

Before I could exit the kitchen, Pam said, "I know you asked him to meet you."

If Pam wanted my attention, she now had it. I did a slow about face and pinned her with a stare.

"What are you talking about?"

"I know you told Elijah to meet you at Bailey's, that sports bar near where Ryan got killed, but you never showed up."

"And How exactly would you know I needed to meet my husband?" I said through clenched teeth.

"It wasn't like that, okay?" Pam replied, disregarding my increasing temper. "He was coming by to get a box of his stuff. It is over between us. He told me he had to change the time he could stop by because you wanted to meet, but when he arrived at my place, he mentioned you never showed."

What a good detective my cousin had turned out to be. Now I see why she got all those awards in school for excelling in academics. She was a great problem solver. Too bad she wasn't smarter than me.

A wicked grin spread across my face.

Pam blinked rapidly and suddenly stood, her hand braced against the top of the chair.

"Did you hurt Ryan, Bree?"

I noticed her voice no longer possessed that high and mighty confidence from earlier. Where had it gone?

"So what if I did?" I asked, a calm settling over me I hadn't felt in a long time.

My words must have truly startled her, because Pam's hand was now tightly gripping the edge of the chair, her knuckles turning white with the force.

The expression on her face was a mixture of shock and disbelief, forming a small O shape with her mouth.

She talked a big game, but my dear cousin wasn't ready to go toe-to toe. Not with me.

"Oh my god," Pam finally said, her hand covering her mouth. "You killed Ryan."

She faced the wall and shook her head frantically, clasping

and unclasping her hands. The woman was going to blow a fuse.

"I... I'm calling the police," Pam said, reaching into her sweater pocket to withdraw her phone.

Now this was a shock!

First she slept with my husband and now she was threatening to turn me in? I thought we had a bond.

It's crazy how quick someone will turn on you if they suspected you of something as frivolous as a little murder.

Evidently, Pam was panic-stricken. However, she was also mistaken if she thought she could call the police on me.

"I wouldn't do that if I were you," I said.

My abrupt response must have bewildered her. Pam lowered the phone and her eyes filled with alarm.

"What are you talking about?"

The dread she emitted was off-putting. Did she believe I planned to physically harm her in some way?

Yes, she deserved a sad ending, but I wouldn't kill her. I didn't even kill Ryan.

"If you call the police, I will say that you and Elijah murdered Ryan so that you could run off together with the money from my software."

Pam slowly shook her head. "No one would believe that."

Yet, I could see that she was starting to.

The hand clutching her phone was lower than seconds before, and I noticed the exact moment it clicked for her.

Giving a person with my level of expertise unrestricted access to her laptop probably wasn't the smartest thing to do.

Especially since I was doing a whole lot more than emailing my divorce attorney.

The evidence I'd planted on Elijah and Pam's computer was enough to put them both under the jail.

Confirming the thoughts that I knew were forming in her head, I said, "They would if I point them to the email exchange that has been going on between you and Elijah for the last several months. I am the victim in all this, you know?"

I don't think I had ever seen Pam more terrified in my entire life, and she was the one that got stuck on the Ferris wheel for two hours when we were eight.

In the minutes that followed, Pam officially blew that fuse I was worried about from earlier. She screamed, cried, and paced so much I thought she might need medical attention.

Admittedly, watching her meltdown was entertaining and satisfying, making me question why I didn't tell her sooner.

"No," she gasped in between agitated sobs, "you're lying."

I walked back to the counter and poured myself another shot. This one was celebratory.

"There's only one way to find out," I answered cooly.

Pam ceased her frantic movements, and we locked eyes. She knew what I was capable of, and I didn't bluff.

Not once I'd gone this far and not once I'd been crossed.

Pam ran out of the kitchen and front door, with her hand over her mouth, strangled cries spilling out the entire time.

I hope she doesn't throw up on my lawn.

Things had looked up, life was back in order and planets aligned.

I felt in control now, better about what was to come, and my happiness soared through the roof when I glanced at the display on my ringing phone.

Well, would you look at that, "R" was calling.

Day 13

THURSDAY
1:38 PM

I sat on the bench at Tribble Mill Park, soothed by a cool breeze on my face and the warm sun on my back.

It was one of my favorite places to bring the kids to let them play, feed the ducks and enjoy a picnic.

There were a lot of excellent memories made at this park, so meeting him here was fitting.

Pulling the small black case I'd brought with me closer to my leg, I rested my hand on it and smiled sweetly as several joggers passed by.

One of them reminded me of Ryan, and I recalled the first time he and I hooked up five months ago.

It was a night that my emotions were at an all-time high. Elijah was out of town, putting work first as usual, and I was home with the kids.

That night, a severe thunderstorm had hit in the area and Ryan had come by to make sure we were okay.

Thankfully, we were. No power outages and no fallen trees.

The kids were asleep, and I hadn't had dinner, so I warmed both of us up a plate and we sat down with a glass of wine and talked.

The wine probably wasn't a good idea, because next thing

I knew, talking became touching and touching became sex in the laundry room on top of the dryer.

It was hot, sweaty and played right into my hand.

"Slow down, Taylor," a woman called, chasing after a little boy that couldn't be any older than two.

He fell down into the grass, got up with a giggle, and kept trotting along. The woman finally caught up to him and the boy squealed with laughter and as a result, I laughed too.

The day was beautiful.

The sun shone brightly in the sky, casting a warm and rich glow over everything. The sky was the perfect shade of blue and birds chirped happily, their melodies filling the air and lifting my mood even higher.

Adjusting my sunglasses, I leaned my head back to rest on the bench and closed my eyes.

I wasn't tired, but with such a serene scene surrounding me, it was a good time to think through the things in my life that had led me to where I currently found myself.

The fact that, for me, all of this began six months ago was hard to fathom.

Although, upon reflection, it was evident that Elijah had been diligently working on his plans long before I heard the whisperings from the other side of his office door.

Regardless, once I'd seen the true face of the monster, I'd married. Wising up and placing a recorder in his office was one of the many smart things I did.

From those recordings, I had heard conversations that revealed a web of deceit, betrayal, and sinister plans that sent chills down my spine.

Conversations Elijah had with lovers, business associates and his best friend...

"I'm going to need you to start up something with Bree to keep her occupied and happy so that she doesn't start suspecting anything." Elijah had said to Ryan.

"Start up?" Ryan asked, his voice rising. *"What do you mean, start up?"*

In my mind's eye I could see his face. That inquisitive, confused look he got that made him look so innocent.

"A steamy affair, a love story, whatever you want to call it. Just keep her out of my hair while I work the details for this deal."

"Hmm," Ryan said, as if to mull it over.

His voice rang out crystal clear through the speakerphone. I expected him to say no, stand up for me, or at the very least, call Elijah out on his shit. Anything except for what he said.

"Bree isn't really my type," Ryan finally confessed.

And Elijah laughed.

"Bree really isn't my type either, and I married her," he said. *"But she is loyal and works hard to keep my interest."*

"Apparently she isn't keeping it that well," Ryan said. *"You couldn't be more disinterested."*

"It's not that I'm disinterested. I just think my marriage has run its course," Elijah offered. *"Don't get me wrong, Bree is smart and reasonably attractive. Plus, she has old-school values and I admire that about her, but I have a big appetite and Bree can't satisfy it."*

"I can't say I don't understand," Ryan replied. *"Ever since college, Bree and I have been good friends. She is a sweet girl, but she's no trophy."*

"Exactly! I will always be grateful for the kids, but I'm done sneaking around. It's time to live my life, and this software is going to let me..." Elijah cleared his throat. *"I mean us, live it phenomenally."*

"Alright then," Ryan said. *"What exactly do you need me to do?"*

"Bree is smart and even though it doesn't show its head often, she has a mean streak," Elijah revealed.

I remembered that comment made me chuckle. *Mean streak?* He had no fucking idea.

"I don't need her catching a whiff of this," Elijah continued. *"She has to stay busy."*

"How busy are you talking?" Ryan questioned. *"You mean, like sex?"*

"Haven't I already made that clear! Whatever works. Truthfully, I don't care."

Ryan laughed again, causing pain and an old familiar darkness that I hadn't felt since Daisy Ramirez, to awaken inside me.

I'd thought it was gone. I was a mom of three now, with a heart full of love and patience. That level of coldness and destruction had disappeared a long time ago, hadn't it?

Turns out my twisted sense of revenge was still there, alive and well. Lying dormant, waiting for me to embrace it and on that day, I did.

"Damn man," Ryan said. *"Do you love her at all?"*

"I love her, but not in the same way she loves me. Besides, I've cheated on her so much this will make her feel like she is getting even. I'm throwing her a bone."

"Okay," Ryan said slowly. *"I can do that, but what should I tell my girl?"*

"What girl?!"

"Kari, you dumbass. We've been dating for two years now." Ryan stated, apparently annoyed that Elijah hadn't remembered.

Elijah laughed him off. *"You're still with her? I thought you broke up with her a while ago."*

"Yes, I am still with her and thinking about proposing soon."

"Big mistake," Elijah said. *"Take it from a man that is already married. It isn't worth it!"*

Ryan dismissed Elijah's advice. *"I'll take my chances, that is, if she will have me once this is all over. If she finds out I am sleeping with Bree, even if it is fake, she will be pissed."*

"Man, do you hear yourself? What if she finds out I'm sleeping with Bree," Elijah said in a tone mocking his best friend. He went back to speaking normally and said, *"Listen, we are about to come into $250 million dollars from this software. If Kari gets that upset with you, just buy her an enormous diamond."*

Ryan blew out a low whistle.

"That is a lot of money. Fuck it, I'm in! When should I make my move on Bree?"

There was a pause, and I heard Elijah shift items around.

"I'm going on a business trip next week. Bree will be home alone and in need of some company. Show up, strike up a conversation and then come on to her."

Ryan exhaled. *"You think she will go for it?"*

"She's a mother of three, and I am barely home," Elijah reasoned. *"She'll be flattered."*

"I'm with you," Ryan said. *"Better brush up on my acting skills so she doesn't know I'm lying."*

"She won't know you're lying, and do you know why?" Elijah said, before stating his favorite quote. *"Because if the devil came knocking, you wouldn't let him in..."*

"Unless he looked like a friend," Ryan finished.

I could practically hear the smile in both their voices.

"You're a sly guy, Elijah Simmons," Ryan said. *"But I like the way you think. Bree won't suspect a thing."*

And neither would they, I remembered thinking.

"While you are keeping her occupied, I will get the divorce set up. By the time she gets served I will be officially living in my condo."

"Ah, that's right! When do you move in?"

"I sign the lease next week. Then I will start moving stuff,

little by little and with football season starting soon, it couldn't be a better time."

That really got Ryan going. *"Sweet! First game at your place?"*

"You buy all the snacks and I'll host."

Ryan laughed. *"Are you going to still be this stingy once the deal clears?"*

"You bet your ass," Elijah snorted with a laugh. *"I'll never change."*

He definitely hadn't changed, so I had to.

My husband and his best friend had their plan. I would be foolish not to devise one of my own.

There were, of course, a few hiccups along the way, Pam not being able to keep her legs shut and the ever-growing amount of pressure that I wouldn't find the software in time.

Despite the challenges, everything fell into place perfectly, and I felt a wave of relief wash over me.

"Hello my Love," came a familiar voice from behind me.

I didn't turn around, because in the movies during the big reveals, the main character always kept the audience on edge a few seconds longer before they unveiled their accomplice.

I was so dramatic, but I loved my old movies.

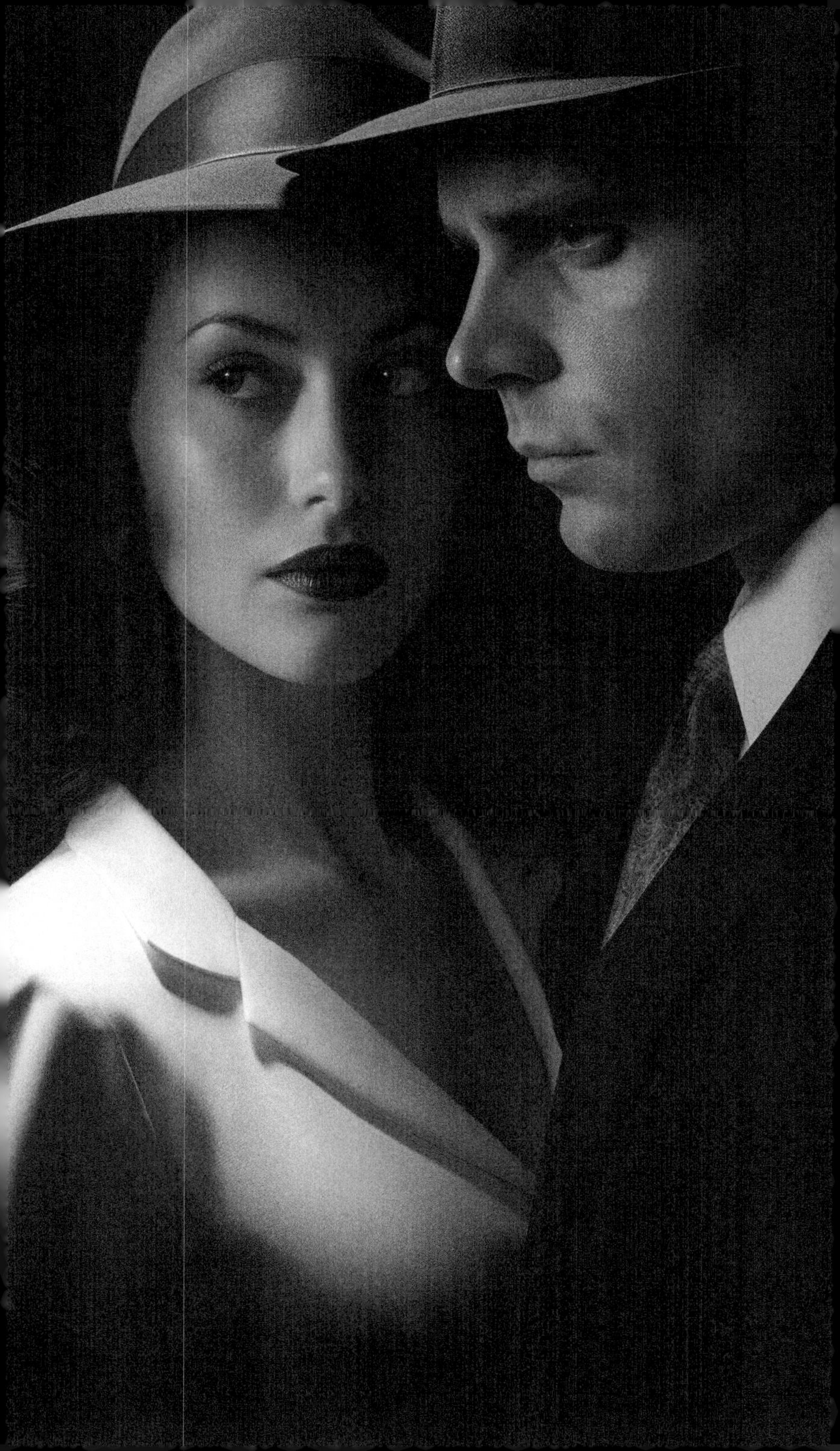

He walked around and sat down on the bench next to me and, at that point, I couldn't resist. I looked over at the man I love... Victor Ramon Grafton, also known as "R."

I always knew that if Elijah got a glimpse of my display screen, he would assume that "R" stood for Ryan. There was no way he would believe that "R" represented the first initial in his boss's middle name.

He viewed me as a pawn in his twisted game, never knowing that I was several steps ahead of him the whole time.

Victor's handsome face was adorned with a smile that exuded warmth, eagerness, and deep satisfaction. I wanted to kiss him so bad, but public affection was a no-no. We had to keep up appearances.

He was wearing a dark blue suit and gray tie, his deep dimples lending him a very boyish charm. Victor didn't look to be in his 50s at all, and he certainly didn't fuck like it.

His eyes dropped to the heart cut pendant that hung around my neck.

"I see you wore my gift," he said.

Instinctively, my fingers caressed the necklace. "I absolutely love it. I was so surprised you didn't forget our anniversary."

"How could I? That was the night I fell in love with you."

It had been four years, and that night seemed like a lifetime ago.

Being the dutiful wife that I was, I'd come to the office to surprise Elijah with dinner, but found Victor instead. Turns out working late for Elijah meant he was having yet another affair.

I broke down and Victor consoled me, leading me to the first time that I ever cheated on Elijah.

During the subsequent weeks, I remained convinced that the entire experience was nothing more than a figment of my imagination.

Yes, I'd noticed the unspoken attraction between Victor and me, but I was a married woman. I could never let my fantasies become a reality.

It's funny how your morals shift when the loneliness and hurt of being an abandoned wife catch up to you.

The opportunity to be embraced, loved and cherished by a man that actually wanted me became too tantalizing of a temptation to resist.

I noticed the box with the Red Zone Sports Agency logo and looked up at him.

"You never miss a step, do you?"

"Not when it comes to caring for you," Victor said.

The box was filled with useless items from Elijah's office.

If someone we knew spotted us, this meeting could be chalked up to the boss giving the wife of his former employee some of his belongings.

Instead of two lovers meeting to discuss the final stages of their plan.

My eyes linger much too long on his perfect lips that intimately knew every part of my body, and I am forced to tear my gaze away.

This was so hard.

For the past six months, we had kept our conversations minimal. In person, phone calls and even texts were reduced drastically.

Until everything was settled with Elijah, I could not be seen touching, kissing, let alone dating Victor. It might raise suspicions.

However, after some time passed, we planned to slowly spend more and more time together in the public, allowing our love story to blossom for the world to see.

I definitely should have left Elijah years ago for Victor. The thought of all the wasted time saddened me. However, Victor always reminds me we can't change the past.

"Has everyone been buying your act?" Victor asked, taking my mind from sex to serious.

"Absolutely! I should get an award for my acting. Gianna believed I was truly heartbroken and had lost my mind over Elijah, and Ryan really thought I believed he loved me."

Victor groaned in disgust.

"I still hate that you slept with him."

"Don't be jealous. I was only playing a role. Every time I got close to him, it helped me to stay in character, knowing I was one step closer to the finish line. But that's over now and he's gone."

"Thinking of him touching you gave me extra satisfaction when I pulled the trigger."

His words gave me goosebumps. I loved Victor so much.

"What about Pam?" Victor asked.

I rolled my eyes behind my sunglasses and patiently waited for a mother to push her baby completely past us before I responded.

"Pam sort of figured it out."

His brow raised. "What do you mean, sort of? Is she going to be a problem?" Victor asked in a no nonsense tone.

I shook my head. I was angry at Pam, but I didn't want her dead. Besides, she wasn't a threat.

"No, I doubt it. Once I hinted at the evidence I'd planted against her, that shut her up. I didn't even have to mention the pictures of her and Elijah that I'd been collecting from the private investigator and Nicole. Also, most importantly she knows nothing about you."

Victor turned to me and since he wasn't wearing any sunglasses, I could see the passion and admiration in his captivating gaze.

His arm rested across the back of the park bench and his fingers inconspicuously caressed my neck. I wanted more of those gentle caresses all over my body, but now wasn't the time.

"Damn, I love you," he said. "That criminal mind of yours turns me on."

"Says the man that killed to defend my honor," I replied with a grin.

Victor's eyes turned dark, and the animalistic edge that initially drew me to him surfaced.

It wasn't like Elijah's selfish nature, willing to hurt anyone as long as he came out on top.

Victor was a patient, gentle soul most of the time, but when someone hurt the ones he loved, all bets were off. That temper of his could be deadly.

"Those bastards not only stole documents to gain access to my investors. They double-crossed and tried to manipulate the woman I love. They got what was coming to them."

His comment reminded me I'd let him down Sunday night. I was supposed to text him to confirm that Ryan was where he should be, but I forgot because the kids and I got sick.

"I know it all worked out, but did you have any trouble finding Ryan that night?"

"Nope, he was exactly where you said he would be, at Val's Sport Bar, watching the game."

"And you were able to avoid being spotted by people or cameras? Did you cover your face? Park far enough away?" I rambled.

I knew we'd took care of the details, Victor more than me, but I couldn't lose him. He was my everything.

"Bree," Victor said, his voice instantly calming me down. "I was careful and I know how to take precautions. This is not my first rodeo, remember?"

I did remember. My love wasn't a stranger to getting his hands dirty.

It was sort of a family business. One that Victor mostly avoided, but the skills were there when necessary. So far, it had been necessary twice.

Well, three times now, counting Ryan.

After a curt nod, I relaxed back onto the bench. "Good, it's done," I said.

"Yes, it is. Ryan has met his maker and Elijah will rot in jail for it."

My sunglasses had slid down my nose, so I pushed them back up.

"Let's hope so. Bridges want's Elijah to plead guilty so that he can get him a deal, but," I said smiling, "Elijah won't take it. He is refusing to say that he killed Ryan."

"Good! His stubborn ways will work in our favor because that plea deal is the only chance he has. Without it, he is going to serve a life sentence. I used his gun, that has his fingerprints, and ditched the weapon where the police would find it."

And they had, along with the testimony of witnesses that spotted Elijah within the area because, yours truly, had requested that he meet me two blocks away from where I knew Ryan would be.

I passed Victor the small black bag that I'd brought with me and he tucked it away inside his jacket pocket.

It was the gun we used as a substitute for Elijah's. The old switcheroo had worked out perfectly!

Right before I confronted Elijah and Pam at Atlas, I'd snuck back into Elijah's office and took his gun from his safe and dropped it off with Victor.

The gun case I saw peeking out from Elijah's bag the day he found out the software was missing and stormed out of the house was not his original gun.

It was the stand in that Victor had given me, so that Elijah didn't know his gun was missing.

I am clueless as to where Victor got the gun. I knew it wasn't his, and I trusted him enough not to ask questions.

Nevertheless, right after Elijah was arrested, I went by his condo and retrieved it. That way, even if Elijah swore to the cops that his gun was at his place, he would look like a madman spitting even more lies.

"What ever happened with the fight at the office between Elijah and Ryan?"

"Exactly what we wanted to happen. Elijah stormed into Ryan's office, accusing him of taking the software. Ryan denied it and Elijah called him a liar and got in his face. From there, temper's flared, and a fight broke out. I called the police and had them both arrested."

"Wow," I said in disbelief.

Elijah fell for my plan so easily. His rapacity drove him and landed him exactly where he belonged, in a cage like the animal he was.

It baffled me that he never once slowed down to think.

How did I even know to find him at the restaurant? Why I never asked him where my software was? And why, after all he'd put me through, would I stand by his side and help him get a lawyer?

Because he was a moron with tunnel vision. Thinking he could float through life unscathed.

Unbeknownst to him, I was secretly listening to his conversations at home, while Victor was doing the same to him and Ryan at work.

"Did you set up new investors with the software?" I asked.

"Yes, Schmidt and Lodges want in on it," Victor said, then he laughed. "Ryan and Elijah were idiots. The software is worth $500 million, not $250 million. However, I will not move forward unless you want me to."

I pondered over it for a long moment.

I really didn't care about the software or the money.

It was like I'd told Gianna; it was the principal of what Elijah had done that had me out for vengeance. I wasn't a sports agent and would never do anything with the software.

"Do whatever you want," I said. "Once I retrieved it from Elijah's hiding spot, I imprinted myself as the creator and gave you the rights to distribute on my behalf."

"Let me know if you ever change your mind," Victor said.

I wouldn't. Besides, I didn't need money.

Two years ago, Victor had given me full financial access and added me as a shareholder to Red Zone Sports Agency. I already had millions in my bank account.

Victor faced me again, his expression signaling that talks of our revenge and malicious natures were over. He had moved on to much happier thoughts.

"Where is my daughter?" he asked.

"Ariel is with my parents. I know you wanted to see her, but as you would expect, things have been crazy at my house. My parents are keeping all three of them until tomorrow."

Victor's hand affectionately slid over mine, as if the thought of not touching me was too unbearable to withstand.

"I love you and Ariel with every fiber of being. And even though Zoey and Grayson are not mine, I love them, too. None of you will ever have to worry about anything."

His sincerity moved me to tears. I loved Victor more than words could describe, and even though I knew he hated when I had regrets about the past, I couldn't help but kick myself.

I should have destroyed Elijah a long time ago.

Day 14

FRIDAY
2:20 PM

"It's a bloodbath," Gianna said, staring straight ahead.

I was inclined to agree. An uneasy feeling rose in the pit of my stomach and I couldn't take my eyes off of it.

Was Ryan covered in blood like that when they found him?

Rapidly blinking, I dismissed the thought. All's well that ends well, and for me the ending would be fantastic.

"Poor goat," I said with a giggle.

"Poor goat, poor workers, poor me," Gianna said. "I have to live with them."

When we brought the kids to Serene Trail Ranch, I thought it would be more... well, serene.

The only peace and joy being had was by the kids. I think the animals and the staff were ready to end their shifts early.

Instructor Gee, an older man with more patience than hair at this point, used a water hose to wash all the red paint off the goat, thanks to Lucia.

This was the first ranch I'd been to that allowed the kids to paint the goats and horses in order to gain a more interactive experience with the animals.

The paint was non-toxic, of course, but the impression it made on the kids wasn't. I'd bet Gianna would have to watch the handcuffs around all cats and dogs from now on.

Already the staff had to tell all three kids to stop running in circles around the animals, to not try to stick their hands in the animal's mouth and to stop pulling the pony's mane so hard.

"Gentle," Instructor Gee had said in a calming whisper. *"We must be gentle."*

That lasted for close to five minutes before Ariel decided it would be funny to slap the pony's ass. Stating that she'd seen it in a cartoon and it made the pony run really fast.

The instructor gave up and moved to a new activity, which was where we found ourselves now.

Gianna and I had decided we, too, needed a new activity, break time.

We'd moved to the bench to watch, rather than be a part of the goat painting project. Instructor Gee was on his own.

Grayson and Zoey were on a guided trail ride that also provided instructions on bridling, saddling, and grooming horses.

They were thrilled and certainly more well mannered than the three busy bodies Gianna and I were watching.

It was a good decision to let them remain out of school for one more day and it was an even better decision to pick them up from my parent's house early.

The children were in excellent hands with my parents, but I was pretty sure keeping three kids for more than one night was a lot of work for two 65-year-olds.

"How are you holding up?" Gianna asked.

I zipped up my jacket and shoved my hands into my pocket. The temperature had been dropping over the last few days and soon I would need to pull out the winter clothes.

"Pretty good."

"Come on, Bree, it's me. Define pretty good."

I laughed.

"Everything really is pretty good. I'm adjusting, which isn't too hard since Elijah was rarely at home, anyway. My biggest focus is the kids. I don't want to cause them any more heartache."

"Trust me, you won't. You're a wonderful mom."

"I am," I said, tooting my own horn.

We shared a laugh.

"What ever happened to lover boy?" Gianna asked, while giving Gia a thumbs up on the yellow and orange goat she painted.

I pursed my lips in agitation.

"I found out that he has a girlfriend," I said flatly. "He's dead to me now."

"As he should be!" Gianna agreed. "Damn men. They are such scum."

Gianna pulled a bottle of water from the small cooler we packed. I nudged her with my shoulder.

"Matteo isn't scum."

She considered it.

"Matteo doesn't want to feel my wrath. If he ever pulled what Elijah did, I would take him for everything. I could not be as forgiving and kind as you have been."

"Yeah, I'm a pushover," I said.

"Don't worry, I still love you. Bleeding heart and all."

"Gee, thanks," I said sarcastically. "You will be happy to know that I have come to a decision about the divorce."

"Please tell me you are going to leave him in that tiny cell and never look back?"

"Yup!"

Gianna gave me a high five. "Go you!," she cheered.

Gianna took a sip of water and zipped up her jacket completely. Realizing I was thirsty too, I grabbed a bottle from the cooler for myself.

"You deserve so much better than Elijah. I hope the next guy you meet will treat you amazing."

I unscrewed the cap on my water.

"I have a feeling I'll get lucky," I said.

"An optimist, I like that. When do you plan to see Elijah again?"

"Tomorrow, I need to touch base about a few things."

"You taking the kids?"

My attention turned to Ariel, slathering her goat with pink paint. When I picked the kids up this morning, I informed them that Elijah had gotten into some trouble and might be gone for a long time.

They seemed a little sad, smiles seemed a little forced, and there was a slight heaviness in their demeanor.

However, it was not as overwhelming as I had initially expected. Despite the sadness, they maintained a level of composure and resilience that surprised me and eventually the conversation moved to happier topics.

Zoey asked if she could spend next weekend at a friend's house. Ariel asked if she could have ice cream, and Grayson wanted to know if he could turn Elijah's office into a dojo for his ninja training in the meantime.

Overall, it was a good talk, and no tears were shed, only a few frowns.

Looks like Elijah's constant absence finally spared them from some heartache instead of adding to it.

"I don't really think jail is a good place to take kids," I ultimately landed on. "Maybe they can write or send pictures if they want."

"That sounds fair."

"Mommy isn't my goat pretty?" Ariel shouted from across the short field between us.

"It's beautiful baby," I said back.

Instructor Gee had called in reinforcements. A younger woman and middle-aged man were now assisting the girls with their creative tasks.

Ariel turned back to her new pink pet, and the woman assisting, had to redirect her from painting the goats eyelashes.

The goat blinked lazily and shifted its head. Disinterested in Ariel's beautification process.

I shook my head and smiled. The grin on Ariel's face reminded me of Victor because it was an exact replicate of his.

My heart filled with love whenever I noticed the similarities between them.

For the most part, Ariel looked like me, but there were those times that I would catch her at a certain angle or making a certain expression and see her father through and through.

When I slept with Victor four years ago, I was unaware that our love child was being created.

Hell, I was so wrapped up in saving my marriage it didn't even dawn on me that Ariel could be Victor's until I was almost six months along.

In my continuous haste to keep my union alive, I had often been sexually active with Elijah, trying to draw his attention back to me and away from other women.

Which was why, initially, the pregnancy brought me so much joy.

I thought another baby would reconnect us. Instead, it pushed us further apart.

Victor reached out to me during my pregnancy, not because he assumed the baby was his, but because he wanted me to leave Elijah and be with him.

Foolishly, I turned him down.

At the time, I'd been married to Elijah for ten years. He was all I knew, and as a devoted wife, it had become my mission to save our marriage.

For that reason, I summoned the strength to tell Victor that our night of passion was a mistake and would never happen again.

Expectantly, Victor backed off and respected my wishes.

That was until I took a paternity test that confirmed Ariel was his daughter.

From there, life took off at full speed and Victor showed up in every way I would allow: asking for photos, having items delivered for the nursery and taking every opportunity to see her.

The man even set up a college fund! And not just for Ariel, but for Grayson and Zoey as well!

He was the epitome of the perfect father. Stepping in when needed, caring for me when times were hard and never pressuring me with ultimatums.

That level of compassion and concern was incredible and welcomed, but it was also new to me, complicated, and produced an enormous amount of guilt.

I was falling in love with Victor and, at the very least, Elijah deserved to know that Ariel was not his.

The problem was, now that I'd had her, Elijah was home even less, leaving me to care for a baby and two other kids.

I was a hormonal and emotional wreck.

Fortunately, over time, things got better and by the time Ariel was two, my stress had lessened and Victor and I were crazy about each other.

The only thing holding me back was Grayson and Zoey. If I left Elijah I'd be uprooting two kids from their father solely based on my feelings for another man.

Wouldn't that make me no better than Elijah?

It sounded selfish, so I stuck to my guns about continuing our affair in secret, at least until they were a little older.

My decision to tough it out ended six months ago when I learned what Elijah had been up to.

It cancelled out all my devotion, guilt, and turned any love left between us to hatred.

Hysterical from shock, embarrassment and deep-seated anger, I told Victor about Elijah's plans to swindle us both.

Victor's response was level-headed, unbothered, and to the point.

"Are you ready to leave him?"

"Yes," I said confidently, my voice laced with intense fury. *"I want him to pay."*

It was all Victor needed to set the wheels in motion and now Elijah, that bastard, would live on his knees.

"What are your plans tomorrow?" Gianna asked, snapping me out of my thoughts.

I considered it for several seconds, as if I didn't know.

"I'm going to get my hair done, a manicure and a pedicure, before I see Elijah in jail."

Gianna was absolutely giddy. "Showing him what he will be missing, huh?"

"It's more for me than him," I said. "Elijah, seeing what he is missing out on is just icing on the cake. By the way, can you watch Ariel tomorrow?"

"Sure thing."

"Mommy," Ariel said, running over to me. "Can we have ice cream?"

I looked at Gianna. "Should we give them sugar?"

"Why not?" Gianna responded, getting to her feet. "I think we should have some, too. We all deserve a treat. Let's live dangerously."

I stood and dusted the dirt from the bench off my jeans.

"Now you're talking," I replied with a grin.

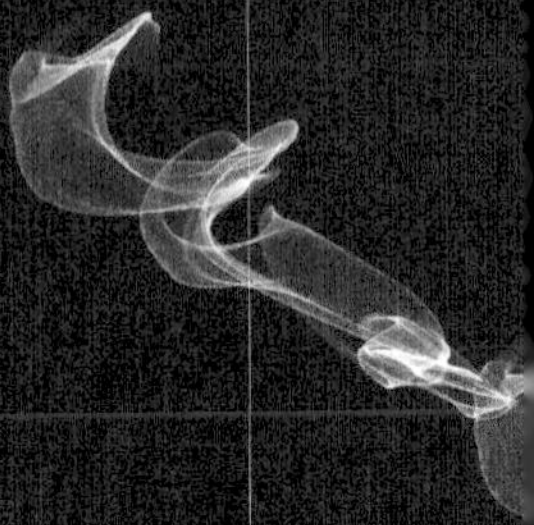

Day 15

SATURDAY
1:14 PM

The diamond butterfly brooch with deep crimson stones, fit perfectly with my beige colored cashmere sweater.

I adjusted it several times to ensure the glistening pin sat perfectly above my right breast.

It astonished me to learn that individuals would pay well over ten thousand dollars for items of this nature.

This brooch specifically was worth $12,000.

It was a gift from Victor, given to him by his grandmother, and I thought it fitting to wear today.

Usually, I preferred dressing a lot more simplistic, but it would be a pleasant change to flaunt my high status from time to time.

My stylish pumps looked like they were worth every bit of the $1000 price tag attached to them.

The shoes supplied me with a three-inch boost that gave my ass the perfect lift in my slim fitted denim jeans, all while being luxuriously comfortable.

I will definitely get more of these.

My hair was modern and tasteful, as I'd gotten it professionally done for the occasion.

The light brown highlights the stylist convinced me to get

were silky and smooth. The perfect touch to complete my overall look.

Not a hair out of place.

As I stood in front of the mirror, marveling at my reflection, I realized that my appearance could be described in a single word: expensive.

To any passerby, I would appear like a woman who was worth a million bucks, and technically speaking, I was. Victor had seen to that.

Elijah had never seen me like this. It would be nice to tease him with what he would never have again.

Making my way downstairs, I entered the kitchen and walked over to the island where a stack of papers that were hand delivered this morning awaited my signature.

I scanned the emboldened line near the top of the first page and smirked.

Petition for dissolution of marriage.

The infamous divorce papers had arrived right on schedule.

Immediately once I received them, I'd taken a seat near my

favorite window and flipped through the stack while enjoying my morning coffee.

From my understanding, Elijah wasn't asking for much at all, which was understandable since, according to his plan, all the real money was to be had after the divorce.

Elijah's signature was already scribbled above his name, and I couldn't help but feel a little disappointed.

This was my marriage summary, a ten-page stack of papers that determined my value within it based on Elijah's perspective.

The good, the bad and the ugly would legally end with one signature. Seemed too simplistic to be effective, and yet, it was all that was required.

In any case, I had already arranged for my attorney to review them and ensure I wasn't getting screwed.

Placing the papers back into the large manila envelope, I collected my purse, keys, and swiftly made my way to the car.

2:18 PM

The drive to the jail was pleasant and quick.

The only thing I held in my hand as I entered the building was the envelope that contained the divorce documents.

Per protocols, I wasn't allowed to bring in my purse or cellphone.

After being cleared through security, an officer by the name of Ollie guided me to the visitation room and told me to sit in area five.

Sliding the chair out, I looked around the small room. It contained ten cut out sections where the visitors could speak to the inmates on a phone and see them through a thick polycarbonate partition.

There was a tiny scratch in the divider in the cubicle where

I sat, but oddly enough, I couldn't tell if it was on my side or the other. A visitor trying to get in? Or an inmate trying to get out?

I imagine it would be excruciating to watch someone you love remain locked in a place like this.

Even worse, if you are an inmate innocent of a crime but forced to live out your days with those much, much worse than you.

Glancing at the clock, I wondered how long it would be before Elijah arrived.

Visitation was only thirty minutes, and even though I definitely wouldn't need that long, I was ready to get this over with.

This place was depressing and disgusting.

The lighting was horrible; the paint was peeling on the walls and dried pieces of gum were stuck on and around the square box I sat in, reminding me of my elementary school days.

Not a good time.

A door on the opposite side of the glass opened, and three prisoners entered the room. Elijah was the third guy in line, and I barely recognized him.

His usual clean-shaven face was now covered in a scruffy beard, adding an air of ruggedness to his appearance. Bags hung under his eyes like weights, and his lips formed a sort of permanent frown.

This place had already begun taking its toll on him. That was... delightful.

I lifted my hand and gave him a slight wave. He hurried over and sat down in the seat, not taking his eyes off of me the entire time.

I bet he liked what he saw.

Picking up the phone, I waited for him to do the same, but

his hand missed it the first couple of times because he was too busy staring at me.

"Bree, you look incredible," he said.

I thanked him for that honest assessment by running my tongue over my lips, then flashing him my most charming smile.

He ate it up.

The gullible man even discreetly reached down and adjusted himself in his orange jumpsuit.

Would you look at that? He was getting turned on.

This was another win for me. To say Elijah had a high sex drive was an understatement.

For at least the last year, he had gone through a box of condoms every week courtesy of his infidelities, so not getting it on the regular would be a nightmare for him.

I held back a laugh as I imagined his dick had to be suffering from withdrawals.

"How are you?" Elijah asked, eyes wide.

And for the first time in a long time, it seemed he actually wanted to know.

"Oh, I'm fantastic!" I said, my smile widening. "But the question is, how are you, Elijah?"

He momentarily studied me, instantly aware that something wasn't right.

The flat, dark edge in my voice clearly threw him, but he needed me, so he brushed it off, leaned in, and answered the question.

"It's crazy in here! The random fights, the disgusting food, and I think they put me in the cell with an actual murderer."

I leaned in close as well.

"Maybe that's because they think you're a murderer, too."

"Bree! I swear…" he began.

With an impatient sigh, I held up my hand to stop him from going off into his declaration of innocence.

"I know," I said. "You didn't kill Ryan."

Elijah's relief was so heavy, he actually curled up as if someone had sucker-punched him in the gut.

"Thank God you believe me! I'm going crazy in here trying to convince them. Bridges is still pushing for that plea deal and I don't get to see a judge about reviewing me for bail again for another two months." He ran his hand through his hair and clutched the phone. "Bree, I can't be in this place for another couple of months."

"I imagine this is hard for you," I said in the same flat tone I'd been using during our entire visit.

And just like the first time, Elijah ignored it, or so I thought. I noticed the way he watched me, questions of uncertainty in his gaze, but like before, it disappeared quickly.

"You have no idea," he said, with exertion.

I narrowed my eyes. Maybe he didn't want to ask me anything for fear that he would upset me and I'd end the visit early. Or maybe on some level, he instinctively knew that he wouldn't like what I had to say.

Regardless, I needed to hurry this process along.

It was almost time for me to meet Victor. He'd booked us a very romantic, very discreet date on his private yacht.

Where we would have staff tending to all our needs, pampering us with spa treatments and serving us dinner.

"I love you, Bree," Elijah blurted out. "Always have and always will."

I didn't respond to his proclamation of love. He would love anyone who came to see him in this hellhole.

Lifting the envelope from my lap, I held it close to the glass for him to see.

"What... what's that?" he asked, confused.

I rolled my eyes. I knew he could see his divorce attorney's name big as day on the label, but I replied anyway.

"This is divorce papers from your attorney that were hand delivered to me this morning."

Elijah shook his head frantically, and I could hear his breathing increase through the phone's receiver. I moved it an inch or two back. His dramatics were far too loud.

"Bree," he began pleading, his free hand rubbing over his beard. "That was a horrible mistake. Something I did on a whim."

"On a whim?" I asked, intrigued.

"Yes! Oh God, Bree. You can't think I'd ever truly divorce you. I was upset when I filed those papers. We'd had a major argument."

"An argument big enough to make you file for divorce without giving me a heads up?" I asked cooly.

"Yes, it was about the kids. You remember, right?" He gave a short laugh, I guess meant to lighten the mood, but the joke was on him.

Using the kids as a cop out was general enough to allow him a weak, yet tangible excuse to attach blame. We consistently argued about the kids, his infidelities and a whole other host of things.

There was no use in asking him to be specific about which argument justified his actions. Therefore, I moved on to my point.

"It doesn't matter how, when or why you filed these papers. You wanted a divorce then so—"

"But I don't want one now," Elijah interjected. "I admit, it was selfish and stupid. I can see that now. By the time we had made up. I had forgotten all about it."

"So you're saying you don't want a divorce?"

I asked in a way that suggested his answer could change my mind, knowing damn well he was getting this divorce. Like it or not.

Nonetheless, I simply couldn't help myself.

Giving Elijah another few minutes of hope before I ripped it all away was much too tempting, especially when a tear fell down his face.

A tear! A fucking tear!

Oh, he was pulling out all the stops. The man hadn't cried in over thirteen years and even then I thought I imagined it.

Elijah only imitated human emotions when he had an angle. Those fake tears were meant to pull at my heartstrings and convince me he was remorseful.

It wouldn't work, but still, I would mark this day on my calendar. It was turning out to be the absolute best.

"I do not want a divorce," he said, enunciating each word so that there was no mistake. "I love you and I could not imagine my life without you. You and the kids are the best thing to ever happen to me. Being in here has given me the chance to think and realize that I have not always been a good husband or father. But from here on out, I am a changed man. I will treat you the way you deserve, Bree, I promise. I am so sorry I ever hurt you. You have to know that."

His groveling skills were top tier and hilarious. He had been in jail less than a week and swore he was a changed man. Unfortunately for him, it was time for me to make my big finish.

I smiled at my soon to be ex-husband.

"I do know that," I said, "Just like I know you didn't kill Ryan."

Elijah placed his hand on the glass, yearning for some form of loving physical contact, even if it were separated by at least six inches of glass.

"You have always been a forgiving and faithful wife, and the fact that you believe me when no one else does is the one thing that keeps me going."

We stared at each other for a long moment, and suddenly Elijah seemed to think about it.

That nagging feeling he may have pushed aside earlier had now returned with a vengeance and he had to ask. Had to understand why I seemed so certain, so calm, so cold.

He sniffed, his hand still on the glass, waiting for me to do the same. "I'm thrilled that you believe me," he said, eyes darting around the room, voice lowering to a whisper. "But with all the evidence stacked against me, how is it you know I didn't kill Ryan?"

And there it was, my cue.

I would not tell him I had been having an affair with Victor for years, that Ariel wasn't his, or that I had millions.

All of those facts could be used against me if he ever convinced an attorney to look in a new direction concerning the case or file for an appeal.

Instead, I had to be subtle, smart, and let him know I'd beat him at his own game in only a way that Elijah would understand.

Placing my hand on the glass to connect with his, I said in a quiet voice, "Because, dear, if the devil came knocking, you wouldn't let him in unless he looked like a friend."

Elijah's expression shifted from contemplation to confusion and then sheer horror as realization hit.

The weight of this newfound knowledge bore down on him and he was paralyzed with fear.

He opened his mouth to speak, but nothing came out. His Adam's apple bobbed up and down as he swallowed repeatedly.

I'd bet anything that those new tears streaming down his face were no longer fake.

My hand dropped from the glass, leaving his frozen in place.

I hung up the phone and stood, blowing him the kiss of

karma before I walked away. My work here was done because my husband... was officially broken.

THE END

If you enjoyed Break Him please leave a 5 star review. It helps me out tremendously.

Also, don't forget to check out more books from my collection!

About the Author

Nicki Grace is an Atlanta native with a bachelor's in business and a Masters in Marketing. As a wife, mother, author and designer, she is addicted to writing, spas, laughing, and sex jokes, but not exactly in that order.

Her comedic personality and unique upbringing by an illiterate but fiercely strong mother and a courageous, prideful father, made her view of the world pretty unconventional.

Luckily for you, someone gave her internet access, and now you get to experience all the EMOTIONAL, EXCITING, SHOCKING, and HOT ideas that reside in her head. She loves to have fun and lives for a good story. And we're guessing so do you! Nickigracenovels.com

- facebook.com/nickigracenovels
- instagram.com/nickigracenovels
- tiktok.com/@nickigracenovels
- bookbub.com/authors/nicki-grace

NICKI GRACE
NOVELS

USE THE QR CODE BELOW TO VISIT MY WEBSITE

Romance

The Inevitable Encounters Series

Book 1: The Hero of my Love Scene

Book 2: The Love of my Past, Present

Book 3 : The Right to my Wrong

The Love Is Series

Book 1: Love is Sweet

Book 2: Love is Sour

Book 3: Love is Salty

Erotica

His Mouthpiece

His Mouthpiece: The Prequel

This Side of Wrong - Coming soon

Thrillers

The Twisted Damsel

Break Him

Women's Fiction

Cut off Your Nose to Spite Your Face

The Splintered Doll (A Memoir)

Self-Help

The TIPSY COUNSELOR Series

The Tipsy Dating Counselor (Summary)

Book 1: The Tipsy Dating Counselor (UNRATED)

Book 2: The Tipsy Marriage Counselor

Book 3: The Pregnancy Counselor